Creeback

When former soldier Jim Rennie finds a dead body at the bottom of Sandy Creek he realizes that his quiet life in Creeback valley is over.

Reluctantly he begins to investigate. The dead boy was not one of the settlers nor a cattleman; nor was he part of their bitter land dispute. Nevertheless, Rennie suspects that the boy's death is central to the feud.

Settlers' homes are being burned and Tom Rutherford, the man responsible, seems too powerful to be stopped. But Jim Rennie knows he must find a way. . . .

Creeback

A. Dorman Leishman

A Black Horse Western

ROBERT HALE · LONDON

© A. Dorman Leishman 2010
First published in Great Britain 2010

ISBN 978-0-7090-8932-2

Robert Hale Limited
Clerkenwell House
Clerkenwell Green
London EC1R 0HT

www.halebooks.com

Typeset by
Derek Doyle & Associates, Shaw Heath
Printed and bound in Great Britain by
CPI Antony Rowe, Chippenham and Eastbourne

CHAPTER ONE

It wanted but an hour till dawn but already the heat was moving, closing in on the county like a fist. Sundown had brought only a little respite from the soaring temperatures, but for an hour there, at about three, it had seemed cooler. Perhaps it was only an illusion, a trick wrought by the darkness and the faintest of breezes. At any rate it was short-lived and already the sun was returning.

Jim Rennie had missed the brief moment of coolness. All through that night he had laboured to help a mare foal down and his task had claimed all his attention. In the stale, overworked atmosphere of the barn he struggled to remember every last detail of medical knowledge gleaned from his surgeon father and desperately reviewed his cavalry experience for any scrap of information, large or small, that would help him here tonight.

As the foal tried to come into the world feet first, and as Rennie tried with every means within his power to bring it round to his way of thinking, he felt at last the returning heat, felt a dull ache between his shoulder blades and knew that he, and the little mare, had very little left to give.

Then, suddenly, it was all over and the baby lay in the straw, head nodding uncertainly during that first, vulnerable half-hour. Rennie conceded as he cleaned its nostrils with straw, that the foal was alive more by luck than good judgement and that brute strength rather than skill had won the day. But they were nevertheless both alive. He felt a ridiculous sense of pride that his rolling stock had been added to by the princely figure of one, and sat back on his heels, happy just to watch the foal find out that if he tried hard enough, those spindly legs of his would hold. When he had finally found his way to his mother and was taking nourishment, Rennie extinguished the storm lantern hanging on the nail behind him and in the darkness was suddenly aware of the oppressive heat.

He let himself out into the yard, drowsy after his exertions but aware that the moment he lay down on his bed he would be unable to sleep for the sultry weight of heat. And anyway, it was almost time for breakfast and another day's work.

At the pump he stripped off his bloody, sweat-saturated shirt and dropped it at his feet, worked the pump handle until water spilled into the basin and drank a little in his cupped hands.

The water at least was cool. He sat on the edge of the trough and leaned contentedly against the metal upright of the pump, gazing at the familiar curve and swell of the valley called Creeback, which was his home. He liked to look at it, to remind himself that this was his and nothing in the world would ever take that sweet skyline away from him, not while he lived anyway. And in the quiet of the night, sitting alone here, it was good to see that solid row of hills marking the boundaries of his property. To the south and east were hills, to the west a short climb and then a steep descent to the nearest town and to the north the ravine that made this valley of his so isolated and so special. On the whole, things were all right with Jim Rennie's world. He would later have cause to look back on that night and wonder at his own complacency.

His gaze turned to the north-west, to the low hills across the ravine. Above these hills the sky glowed and throbbed a faint shade of pink, a soft blush that suffused the northern sky. He watched this hovering, strengthening glow for some time before realizing that he was facing the wrong way.

That was not the dawn, not the returning sun. Beyond that ravine and those hills was a settlement worked by his friend Sam Cutter and that colour in the sky had to be fire. He snatched up his shirt and put it on as he ran for the corral, his eyes fastened all the time on the warm light, telling himself that a fire of such proportions could mean that Sam's entire place was ablaze. He whistled through his teeth and his horse, an elderly and scarred buckskin, came like a pet dog. He made do with a halter and rode out of the yard and up the valley trail, hatless and bareback, his noisy passage across the slatted wooden bridge that straddled the ravine sending echoes deep into the warm darkness below. On the rise above Sam's place he stopped to look down. There was only one building burning and it was the barn. Just the same, it was the biggest bonfire Rennie had seen since they burned Atlanta. Well, almost. Certainly it had attracted a crowd, most of Sam's immediate neighbours and friends. Unable to sleep for the heat, they had seen the fire and had come to help, unhesitatingly.

But on the slope above the Cutter place, Jim Rennie hesitated. He could include himself as one of Sam's friends, for they had fought all the war years side by side, but since his arrival in this part of the world Rennie had made it a policy never to become involved in anything that might happen this side of the ravine, in fact in anything that might happen outside of his own little valley. But now he hesitated, wanting to help and to ignore his own instincts, which were always very sound. If it had been anyone else but Sam he would have turned and gone home without a backward glance. But it wasn't anyone else. It was his oldest and closest friend and with a murmured, 'What the hell,' he rode down the slope.

7

He dismounted while still a little way beyond the front yard and sprinted the remainder of the way, buttoning his shirt as he ran, squinting his eyes against the glare and the acrid, burning smoke. Amidst the noise and confusion, a bucket brigade was tirelessly feeding water to the red giant, whose roar and bellow made nonsense of their efforts. Sam Cutter, lately the owner of the doomed building, swung round to take another bucket of water and spotted Jim Rennie. His heart gladdened at the sight of him, even though most of his good friends and neighbours were already here. In a crisis Jim Rennie was worth six other men.

'Am I glad to see you!' he said and Rennie nodded, turning slitted eyes to the burning barn.

'You Cutters never do anything by halves,' he grinned and despite himself, Sam grinned back.

'That's a fact. Didn't think you could see it clear across to Creeback though.'

Rennie's eyes expressed regret at this happening to Sam of all people.

'Everybody in the territory knows you got trouble, Sam.' And he was already running to join the ragged chain of men, women and children trying to fight the fire, hauling water buckets next to an awestruck boy who kept up a running commentary on the size, smell and taste of that fire.

They were too late to save the barn structure, but there was an obvious danger to the house and other buildings from sparks and cinders, for everything was tinder-dry. So the volunteers worked slavishly, with buckets and stirrup pumps and shovels full of earth and in the end the stubborn, flaming mass of deadly rage collapsed in on itself, sending showers of red and orange sparks shooting into the sky. The colossal heat that had held the firefighters at bay and had baked their skin till they could not bear it a minute longer, suddenly died, a spent force.

Rennie dropped the bucket he was holding and turned his flame-seared eyes away. It was morning. The sun had risen quite unnoticed, its soft arrival upstaged by the melodramatic performance of the fire. Now they all stood in silence, looking at the desolation before them. Those who were familiar with the sight of the barn found it strange to be able to see the space on the other side, a tree and rock knoll they had never seen from this angle before. The hole it left in the horizon was disturbing. Men picked their way through the wreckage, turning over blackened timbers in search of hot spots, ready to douse them.

Rennie walked aimlessly across the yard, looking for his horse, wondering if he looked as filthy as he felt. In fact, he looked like a front-line veteran who has spent the night between shells and ditch. He remembered now that he had turned the buckskin loose at the foot of the hills. He turned in that direction, only to find his path barred by a fellow fighter, equally smoke-smudged but altogether prettier. Eve Cutter was Sam's only daughter, a girl of twenty, black hair tangled and clinging in soft tendrils to her cheeks. She regarded Rennie coolly and offered him a cup of coffee. Rennie's heart gave mutinous lurch at the sight of her, though his 'Thank you' was only civil and his little nod merely polite as he accepted the coffee from her.

'Why, Mr Rennie,' she said innocently, 'we didn't expect to see you here.' Rennie sipped his coffee and admired her eyes, which were blue as clear pond water.

'Why not, Miss Cutter,' he asked, equally innocently.

'We thought you were our fence-sitter hereabouts.' Her insult was delivered in the cool tone of someone discussing the weather and Rennie checked a little sigh of dismay. He did not want to argue with her. It had been two weeks since he last caught a glimpse of her across the street in town, and this morning he wanted just to look at her, exchange a quiet

9

word or two, but she was spoiling for a fight and he tried, at first, to avoid the confrontation she sought.

'I like to mind my own affairs,' he said evenly and the girl gave an attractive little shrug.

'Then why come?'

'Fire is a common enemy, Miss Cutter.'

'And if it had been Tom Rutherford's barn burning? Would you have gone there?' she asked in a quickened voice, for she thought she had at last said something to this man that would provoke a response in him other than politeness. But she had already missed the glinting stud of humour in his eyes.

'I couldn't have seen a fire that far away unless I'd been invited to dinner. I'm not on dining terms with Mr Rutherford.'

Eve searched around for a weapon to combat his maddening impassiveness and found one.

'Oh come now, Mr Rennie. Surely that's only a matter of time.' She saw him stiffen, his lips tightening down on anger held back and she realized that her weapon had been a little too blunt. And she also knew that she had no right to say such a thing. There was no reason to suppose that Jim Rennie was any friendlier with Rutherford than anyone here this morning. As he returned the coffee cup, she risked a glance at his eyes. What was that look there, that half-veiled look that she did not understand? She had seen it before and it disturbed her for Rennie was no country boy, green as corn as most about here and that she was on dangerous ground when she goaded him. There would be a point beyond which it would not be safe to push him.

Sam Cutter intervened at this point. Turning to look at them he saw that Eve had that tight-lipped look of a woman giving a man a hard time and Sam guessed, from knowing his daughter's honest but impulsive tongue that she had made some comment on Rennie's neutrality. Cutter had no fear that she might have hurt the man's feelings, but that she might have squashed any hopes of winning him over to the settlers' side. There was a fight looming and an army man like Rennie, an officer with leadership skills and great personal courage, would be worth his weight in gold to these people. He strolled towards them, a tired smile on his grimy face.

'It's been a long night,' he said and he saw it now, the look on Rennie's face of anger frozen and held in place by good manners and Eve, flushed with having said too much and maybe not enough.

'I should be getting home,' Rennie said, and he turned to Eve, his voice and face quite expressionless.

'Thank you for the coffee.' He bowed his head courteously to her and she nodded, smiled at her father and turned away, tossing the dregs from his cup into the dust as she went to join the others. Rennie watched her go and felt as if his heart were in a vice.

Sam spoke and Rennie turned.

'Want to thank you for coming, Jim.'

Rennie looked at the charred ruin of the barn. Smoke rose in delicate streamers from the ashes and the air was acrid still with the stink of it.

'Save your thanks for Mother Nature, Sam. She was awful kind to you last night.'

Sam surveyed the wreckage and knew that in a pinch he would have a new barn up by harvest, providing some fresh calamity did not befall him before then.

'I know. Just a light breeze . . . well, I guess we both know what that would have meant. What worries me though is that it might not have been an accident. In fact I'm damned near sure it wasn't.'

Rennie nodded with genuine sympathy but he had no wish to go down that road again, the one that led to involvement with the settlers and making all his old mistakes again. He had just covered that ground with Eve and his mouth was dry with the dust of it. He diverted Sam from his bleak speculations by mentioning the birth of the foal.

'Some good news at last,' Sam laughed. 'Did she give you any trouble?'

Rennie started to tell him the whole story but was frankly too tired.

'Nothing to speak of,' he shrugged. 'They're both fine.'

'Good. I'll drop by sometime and see the youngster.'

'You know I'm always glad to see you, Sam.'

'But you'll stay for breakfast?'

Rennie hesitated, the smile fading from his face.

'I'll keep Eve out of your hair, I promise,' Sam said with a grin. At the mention of her name, Rennie looked towards the house where Eve was dispensing coffee. His eye as it rested on her was gentle and for the first time Sam really saw the way his old friend looked at his daughter. He struggled to interpret its meaning and puzzlement shifted across his eyes.

'Well, I'll be damned,' he said under his breath. Rennie did not hear him. He ran fingers through his dirty hair several times then let his arm fall at his side and gave a little dog-tired sigh.

'Thanks anyway. I'd better get back and see how my family's doing.' They shook hands and Rennie turned and walked slowly up the rise towards his grazing horse. Sam gave his head a thoughtful little shake as he watched his young friend leave. 'I'll be damned,' he said again, aloud this time and rubbed a big hand across the back of his tired neck.

The buckskin came to meet Rennie on the slope and after fussing with him for a minute, a ritual of murmured endearments and chest stroking which the old horse loved, Rennie swung stiffly up onto his back and turned for home.

He was still a little bit disturbed by the accusing look in Eve

Cutter's eyes, a look that filled him with a sense of regret because since the first day he had set eyes on her, he had been her slave, nothing more nor less than that. But he had always been able to hide those feelings outwardly. His logic in the matter was impeccable. He was too old for her and he was unwilling to become part of the Rutherford feud. Rennie had no quarrel with Tom Rutherford, owner of the huge cattle spread to the east. Rutherford might want the tract of land the settlers had claimed, quite legally, as their own, but he had shown absolutely no interest in crossing the natural barrier of the ravine to Creeback, and so long as it stayed that way, Jim Rennie would remain neutral. Even his love for Eve Cutter was not enough to involve him in a fight he had no part of.

At the top of the rise he looked back. He saw the dead black square where the barn had burned so feverishly and around the house, eating casually from plates balanced on knees and drinking coffee from cups held in smoke-blackened hands, the settlers ate a well-earned breakfast, attended to by a slender, black-haired girl who, as if sensing his look, turned in his direction. He wondered now why he hadn't stayed for he could smell bacon frying and he was suddenly really hungry.

Eve shielded her eyes with her hand as she looked up at the man on the ridge. She could feel his gaze touching her and if Eve had disturbed Rennie, then he had left an impression as wide as a highway on her thoughts. His eyes, she recalled, were blue, the colour of hot smoke. His hair was brown, long on the collar, with a dark slat of it inclined to fall over his brow. He didn't smile much but when he did, his smile radiated warmth and charm. He had a wonderful smile, Eve decided. But the man himself was as distant as those purple mountains on the horizon, always in sight but actually very far away, unreachable perhaps. She regretted now not having made him more welcome because he had stepped out of

13

character by coming and she had been a little less than civil to him.

He was her father's oldest friend. They had fought through the war side by side, when Cutter had been a top sergeant and Jim Rennie his captain, which seemed odd to Eve because her father was older. But the differences in age, education and background had made no difference to a friendship that had survived Bull Run and emerged intact at Gettysburg. Even though Sam had immediately taken his family west when the war was over and Rennie had continued with his military career, the bond between them had remained unchanged, had grown quietly strong, even when they were separated, so that when Jim Rennie arrived to take over Creeback Valley, quite by chance close to Sam, it was as if they had never been apart. Even Rennie's reluctance, indeed his downright refusal, to be a part of the Rutherford fight did not affect Sam. He appeared to understand something about Rennie that no one else did. He understood it and accepted it and his affection remained undiminished. Eve wanted to understand too. Caution and unwillingness to fight she could understand from men who had never done anything more dangerous than hunt squirrel but not from a soldier, a man trained to face danger. He turned and was gone from the skyline and Eve sighed, her slight shoulders dropping with her own sudden fatigue as she returned to the house.

Rennie cleared the slight slope above Sam's place and crossed down to the track below, letting the buckskin find his own way and as they veered around and down to the wooden bridge, something made him glance back. On his left, under some cottonwoods, three men, half-hidden by low foliage, were watching the Cutter place. Rennie recognized two of them as Rutherford cattlemen, but the third was a stranger and his head and shoulders were so heavily shaded that he could make nothing out of his features. Around his neck, dangling almost to the waist on a stout metal chain was an ornate but cheap-looking crucifix. There was something vaguely familiar to Rennie about this man, about the way he slouched forward in the saddle, but fatally, he did not pursue the memory. Clearly they had seen the fire on their way back from town and had come to gloat. He wheeled and cantered home, put the buckskin into the corral, looked in on the new foal, which was doing nicely thank you and then took himself off to bed for an hour or two, tearing off and finally ridding himself of his filthy, blood-stained, smoke-blackened shirt. He slept deeply and dreamlessly until noon.

CHAPTER TWO

Late that afternoon, Rennie saddled the buckskin to ride to town for a few supplies, but mainly for coffee, which he had been doing without for a week. Alexander was the closest town, being just a little over three miles away and was reached by a broad, well-used track that sloped steeply down and then across Sandy Creek where there was no sand, the river bed being mostly gravel and stone. It had been named by the same man who founded the town. His name was Alexander Anderson and he had built the first hotel and the Baptist church and school, had opened the first bank and had laid three streets with wooden pavements. He had even been to Creeback, with the lofty idea of starting another settlement there, but wisely decided against it and left the sweet little valley alone, not even bothering to change the name the Indians had given it, for he thought it curiously logical. Creeback did geographically sit at the back of the creek, though the Indian name meant something else entirely. When he died all he had passed to three sons and a daughter. His sons were variously a lawyer, a newspaperman who printed the local news-sheet and a politician, who more or less lived in Washington. Though no longer as powerful as their father had been, they still had a steady finger on the pulse of their father's town. They were the quiet, softly-spoken men of influence, who watched but mostly did not intervene. It was from the lawyer, Arthur Anderson, that Rennie had taken out the lease on Creeback.

The sapping, suffocating heat of the day had slackened and it was cool here, with plenty of tree shade and the cool rush and sparkle of the water. The track that led down to the stout wooden bridge was steep and as Rennie swayed downward, the molten flicker of sunlight through the branches struck his face and made him feel pleasantly drowsy. On the bridge he dismounted to lead his horse across and he paused, admiring the scenery. It was a pretty spot, with willows dipping down to the fast-flowing creek. He leaned on the parapet and felt the cool updraught of water spray on his face. It was good, reassuring, to see an abundance of water during such a hot, dry spell. Of course the creek had never been known to slacken its surging, unchecked journey to the town, which was one of the main reasons why Alexander, sometimes known to his intimates as Sandy, had chosen the little valley that this river emptied into to build his town. Rennie closed his eyes and for a minute toyed with the idea of plunging into that cold, clean water, the sharp current washing the dust and sweat away. When he opened his eyes again, something on the right-hand bank caught his attention, a flash of something metallic that did not fit with the fern and reed there. For a moment, in idle fashion, he stared at the odd shape and suggestion of greenery. Then all at once his eye made sense of it. He straightened from the parapet and vaulted the rail, landing upright in four feet of rapidly moving water. He struggled to the right-hand bank, slipping on rocks scoured smooth by the constant passage of water, and jostled by the boisterous current that only a moment ago had seemed so inviting.

What he had seen was a man, dangling upside down, his head and shoulders in the creek, his hips and legs arrested by the fork of a tree branch. Standing hip-high in the water, he

17

lifted the man down, hauling his waterlogged upper half onto a flat area slightly upstream from where he had initially come to rest. Rolling him onto his face on the grass he began the only form of resuscitation he knew, which was to press down with both hands on the back, to try to push the water out of his chest physically. But as he pressed he saw a slash in the fabric of the shirt, about six or eight inches long, and under that a matching slit in the man's back, just under the left shoulder blade. The wound was no longer bleeding, but it had bled considerably when first inflicted. The back and sleeve had been saturated, the blood where the water had not washed it still tacky. Rennie sat back on his heels. The man was dead, but not from drowning. No, he did not have a drowned look, Rennie saw, as he turned the body over to look at a young face, hardly mature and in death surprised, the mouth forming a small, white-lipped 'o' of surprise. Rennie knew the face. It belonged to a young man named Corey. Rennie thought his first name might be Ben but could not remember how he knew him. Rennie looked up the sharp slope to the edge of the creek. It was obvious that he had fallen or been pushed from the lip there. Another few feet and he would have hit the water, might have been carried into the next county before anyone found him.

He turned and climbed, a hard, difficult scramble that left him sweating and breathing hard as he finally heaved himself up onto the edge. He turned carefully to look down at the boiling creek and the doll-like figure on the bank and he wondered what had brought Corey to this place. This spot was yards from the main trail and led nowhere. He must have been dragged and dropped or perhaps a fight that started on the trail had ended here, with a knife and a cry and plunging drop of forty feet. Cuffing sweat from his nose, Rennie made his way back along the trail, his downcast eyes noting the double set of tracks, the imprint of a heavy sole, as of

18

someone hefting a load and the other of a pair of dragging heels. And just off the main trail, where the grass was churned and trodden with signs of a struggle, the first blood had been drawn.

Rennie descended the easy way, via the winding trail and since there was no other course open to him, waded back to the body and carried it to the bridge. He packed the luckless Corey across the saddle with speed and an expertise born of his army years, and the buckskin stood with patiently bowed head, too well disciplined to be skittish at the smell of blood. The bundle on the saddle, once wrapped in Rennie's saddle blanket, looked strangely pathetic and he stood for a moment with his hand on the young man's back, moved suddenly by the sadness of the burden.

He continued the journey to town on foot and as he walked he thought about the reasons for this murder, for murder it undoubtedly was. The settlers had only one real enemy. Tom Rutherford. He did not want them on land he had always presumed to be his own and he was prepared to do just about anything to persuade them to move elsewhere, including burning Sam Cutter's barn to carbon. But Ben Corey was no settler, Rennie thought, struggling to recall something more about the boy. He worked somewhere in town, he was sure, though he thought that perhaps his mother owned a smallholding west of Sam's property. It was entirely likely, of course, that Corey had died for reasons that had nothing to do with the range dispute currently occupying everyone, but not very likely. As he plodded up the gradient into town he dismissed all speculation. In the first place it was none of his concern. He would turn the matter over to the sheriff and go home. As for the reasons for Corey's death, Rennie knew that there were men on this earth who needed no reason to kill other than a liking for it. He had seen enough of that during the war, more than his fair share of the

19

sight of innocent young faces, younger even than Ben Corey, in death, murdered on the word of some desk-bound, beribboned general or other to gain a few yards of blood-sodden ground.

A hand tugging on his arm drew him back from his bloody recollections and he turned, saw Andrew Cutter walking, half-running beside him. Andrew was Eve's younger brother, black-haired like his sister and with his father's square-cut, honest face.

'What you got there, Jim?'

'Nothing for you to worry over, Andy. Your dad in town?'

'Yes, sir. He's at the lumber yard.'

'Run fetch him for me,' he asked and as Andy sprinted off Rennie found that he had a little knot of curious townspeople following him, forming questions.

'Who is that, son?'

'That anybody we know?'

'Where'd you find him?'

Rennie smiled politely, because his mother had taught him always to be polite, and walked on in silence to the sheriff's office. He tethered the buckskin and leaned his back on the hitching post, arms patiently folded, watching as the restless onlookers fell to useless speculation amongst themselves. Rennie stared at them blankly and tried to remember what he had come to town for in the first place, remembered that it was coffee he needed, just as a breathless, grim-faced Sam Cutter arrived.

'Jim? Andy said you'd a—' He stopped, seeing the body rolled in the blanket and packed over the horse. The boy's boots protruded at one end of the expertly secured load. 'A dead body with you. Dear God, who is it?'

'I think his name is Corey. Ben Corey.' Rennie said quietly and blink for blink Sam's reaction was the twin of his own, surprise, disbelief and then sadness.

'Young Ben?' He lifted a corner of the blanket and saw the head hanging down, river water running still from his hair. 'Why, the boy's wet. Did he drown?'

'Sam,' Rennie cautioned and he looked around, seeming to see the watching faces for the first time. 'I thought maybe you could take him over to Doctor Garson for me, while I talk to the sheriff.'

With a hundred questions to ask, Sam gave a nod, took the reins and turned to cross the street. In the jail house, Sheriff Cass was eating his supper. He looked up when Rennie came in but continued eating, cutting his meat, forking it to his mouth and chewing slowly. Between mouthfuls of food he swallowed beer from a jug at his elbow.

Rennie sat down uninvited in a chair on the other side of the desk, the rather slow movement betraying a weariness in him that had a lot to do with the heat and a little to do with the unexpected sight of violent and sudden death.

'This a social call or what?' Cass asked, his mouth half full.

'I found a body in the creek.' Rennie said bluntly and Cass nodded, not surprised, not shocked.

'Was he drunk?'

'Couldn't say. Why?'

'Fished a fella out of the crick last year. He was drunk, wandered off the track. It's pretty steep up yonder.' He spoke the words dispassionately, hardened to the facts of drunks and steep-sided creeks. Rennie wondered if Cass was from Tennessee. His accent was almost the same as a young corporal he had known, another dead boy, killed by a crazed horse jumping on him as it desperately tried to flee the din of battle. Rennie closed his eyes and let the memory come and go, sweat gathering on his lashes and then stinging his eyes when he looked again at Cass.

'Who was it, anyway?'

'I think his name is Corey.'

'Oh, yeah. One of our sodbuster friends.'

'What's that supposed to mean?'

'They're a bunch of trouble, that's what I mean, them and Rutherford. I wish they'd *all* go drown in the crick.'

'Well, first of all it wasn't George Corey I found. It was Ben. He worked here in town somewhere so far as I know, so he's no sodbuster, though I think his mother has a place not far from Sam Cutter. Second, he didn't drown.'

Cass smiled unexpectedly, a grim smile that never touched his dark, humourless eyes.

'I thought you liked to keep your nose out of other people's business, Rennie,' he remarked.

'I couldn't have left him there,' Rennie said, a simple statement of fact. Cass finished the last of his beer, pushed his plate away and stood up, shaking his head.

'I don't see why not. You've managed to ignore just about everything else that's been going on since you got here.'

Rennie stood up too. He didn't care what the sheriff thought of him and he was too tired to get into name-calling but he suddenly had a bad feeling that bringing Ben Corey out of Sandy Creek had been a mistake.

'Nevertheless, I did bring him here and if you want to take a look at the hole in his back that somebody's knife made, Sam Cutter's just taken the body to the doctor's office.'

Cass reached for his hat and sat it casually on the back of his head.

'All righty,' he said pleasantly. 'Since you went to the trouble of bringin' him here an' all. Let's go see.'

Rennie waited on Doctor Garson's front porch while Cass went inside. The curious townsfolk had gone home and the street was quiet, evening beginning to blur the edges of the buildings as the sky softened from metallic blue to mauve and then indigo. Somewhere a pot roast was cooking and from a window above the porch the familiar aroma of coffee reminded him again of the simple errand he had set out on earlier today.

The door at last opened and Cass came out followed by Sam and then the doctor, rolling down his sleeve with an abstracted air. The doctor was also from Boston, a burly, fair-haired man with a drooping moustache, big, square, capable shoulders and fine, delicate hands. He lit the porch lamp and then balanced a hip on the railing beside Rennie. Sam and the doctor were the two closest friends he had and tonight they both looked like worried men. Sam stood uneasily beside him, hands in his pockets. Cass leaned against a post and began building himself a smoke. He seemed taken up with this for a time until he spoke, suddenly directing his gaze at Rennie.

'Just a boy,' he said, with a shake of the head. 'Sad to die that young.'

Sam and the doctor nodded and murmured agreement and for no good reason the hairs on the nape of Rennie's neck began to crawl.

'Tell me again, Jim, how you found him?' Cass asked.

With a little pause, wondering where this was going, Rennie answered.

'I was crossing Sandy Creek Bridge. . . .'

'When?'

'About six I'd say. Why?'

Cass put away his tobacco pouch and hung the cigarette on his lip, but let it hang there unlit.

'Well, it's just that Sam here crossed that bridge with his boy at six o'clock exactly and he says for sure there was nobody on the bank at that time.'

'Meaning what?' Rennie asked tersely.

'Meaning this. If he wasn't on the bank at six, he must've bin brought there just minutes after Sam and Andrew crossed over.'

Digesting this uncomfortably, Rennie knew how lame it

23

would sound to say that he could have been wrong about the time. It had taken him about half an hour to fetch and secure the body and he had walked into town. But the accusation written in Cass's eyes was plain.

'I didn't see anybody,' he answered the accusation, but Cass ran on as if he had not heard.

'Now we all know your position hereabouts, Jim, how you don't get involved an' all. Wouldn't it be fair to say that you might not want to tell us if you saw the boy's killer?'

Rennie worked a minor miracle and battened down his temper, pinning it firmly to the logic of his reply.

'I could have ridden on, left him there. I could have let somebody else find him.'

'That's right, Cass,' Sam intervened hotly. 'There's no call for you to make accusations like that.' Sam could not forget that Rennie had offered help this morning when he could have held it back. He could not forget the man Jim Rennie was anyway. He might turn a blind eye on a fight that he neither started nor cared to join, but he would never shut his eyes to murder. And anyway, Sam was feeling a little bit guilty for putting Rennie in the frame, albeit unintentionally.

'All I'm sayin' is, if you didn't see the killer, then you didn't see him by much.'

A muscle under Rennie's eye trembled as he checked the urge to punch Cass on the nose.

'I didn't see anything,' he repeated. 'Not a jackrabbit. Just a body and some tracks at the top of the creek. Go look at them, Cass, because they'll tell you more than I can.'

'All right Jim, we'll let it ride for now. But if you happen to remember anything, you know where to find me.' He gave a Rennie a last, long look from a pair of impassive black eyes and then turned on his heel and stepped soundlessly off the porch steps into the dust, crossing the street with a casual, easy sway of his big shoulders, a sinister gracefulness in his stride despite his height and power. He might put on a show of cynical indifference to the world, but Cass cared about his town, his community and about the settlers and he had become increasingly angry about the behaviour of the Rutherford crowd. He was not a man Rennie wanted for an enemy.

'I swear I didn't see a soul,' he said almost to himself. Doctor Garson and Sam came to stand beside him. They smiled at him reassuringly, Sam giving his shoulder a brief, fatherly squeeze, neither man believing what Cass believed. Rennie wished that were a comfort to him.

'Forget it, Jim. That's just his way. Come on, I'll buy you a drink.' Sam offered. Rennie gave a little nod and the three men crossed the street. Sam gave a shrill whistle towards the direction of the lumberyard and Andrew came running. Sam caught his son playfully round the neck and rubbed his knuckles on the boy's skull.

'Can I have a beer too, Dad?' he asked.

'Sure, son. And a whiskey chaser if you want.'

Realizing he was being ragged, Andrew started boxing Sam, throwing little jabs at his father's unflinching body. Sam boxed back, landing soft blows on Andy's head.

'What was it you came into town for anyway, Jim?' he asked, ending the mock fight by lifting Andy up and tucking him under his arm like a sack of potatoes. Smiling at the interplay between father and son, oddly comforted by the normality of it, Rennie gave a deep sigh.

'Damned if I can remember.'

CHAPTER THREE

Three days later he rose earlier than usual, resolved to clear a piece of land he had been thinking about tackling for some time. He cooked himself a working breakfast and ate it on the porch with one eye on the sun, already climbing murderously into a brassy sky, and the other on the valley road. Earlier, he had thought there was someone, a rider, coming down the trail, but now as he scanned the slope, he decided he had been mistaken. He fetched his axe from the woodshed, crossed the little stream at the edge of the meadow and, on the other side, spat on his palms and set to work levelling two dead trees that made the property unfit for ploughing. He wanted to cut away as much root as possible before attempting to pull the stumps.

The sky remained clear and cloudless through two hours of solid work and the sun crept up over his shoulder and watched with a hot, baleful stare as he drove the axe rhythmically into the weathered wood. The first tree, which had never reached full maturity before being fired by lightning, conceded its hold on the patch of ground it occupied with a deal of reluctance. Rennie put his shoulder to it and it toppled with a dry crunch into the dirt. Pausing to drink water from his canteen, he peeled his shirt and moved on to the next.

As time passed, he became aware that he was being watched, but he continued to swing the axe against the tree bole, his stroke steady and unbroken. And then a rider came into his line of vision, stepping almost casually out of the corner of his eye and crossing to the space opposite. Rennie stopped, straightened up and looked directly at his visitor. It was a woman, dark-haired, dark-eyed, wearing a green velvet riding habit and a snowy-white blouse. After several seconds of being appraised by a not very friendly pair of dark-blue eyes, she spoke to him.

'It's Mr Rennie, isn't it?'

'Rutherford must have paid a lot for that accent,' he said, recognizing without much difficulty the daughter of Tom Rutherford, his only child, pampered and spoilt, educated in New England and France, taken on the Grand Tour and brought back to earth with a thud on returning to her father's domain. Heat, dust, flies, cattle and people who spoke in monosyllables. After the Champs Elysées, it was a little hard to take in. But occasionally there came a dark horse on the horizon, a man who handled an axe as if he had been born with one in his hand, and yet who had been to good schools and had seen the same sights in Europe as she and had the same flat-vowelled accent as she did. Yet she knew that all these similarities did not put Jim Rennie on her side of the fence. Clara Rutherford gave him a little nod of recognition however, before responding to his question.

'He paid a lot,' she agreed. Time passed. She made no further move to speak or to offer a reason for her presence, uninvited, on his property and so Rennie lifted his axe and resumed his stroke. After the third blow, she condescended to speak again.

'Mr Rennie?' Again he halted, lowering the blade and giving her his undivided attention.

'Yes, ma'am.'

She was not sure how to treat this particular brand of insolence, for there was insolence in his blue eyes and apparent politeness. At home she had the power to deal with it, swiftly and surely, but today she must play the part of diplomat and friend.

'I heard a boy was killed. One of the settlers.' She waited.

Rennie looked at her quietly with no expression on his face, save perhaps a touch of puzzlement and no answer on his lips.

'And ... that you found him. Please correct me if I'm wrong.' Rennie looked at the tree, leaning drunkenly to one side. He placed the sole of his boot against it and the blackened timber submitted, falling slowly and noisily in a shower of splintering, rotten wood.

'I won't correct you, Miss Rutherford. No need for it.' He lifted his shirt and dried the sweat on his chest and arms, stooped to pick up the axe and started back to the house. Clara watched his receding back with astonishment.

At the stream he stopped to soak the shirt in the cool, clean water and as she dismounted to follow him on foot she saw him press the cloth to his face and then walk on to the house with it draped around his neck. In the yard she looked around, noting the orderliness of everything and in the corral a mare with a few days' old foal. Rennie had meanwhile changed his shirt. He came onto the porch and down the steps towards her.

'You found the boy, did you say?' she asked him again. Rennie buttoned the shirtfront and then with slow deliberateness the cuffs, not to rile her, but to give himself time to think. What exactly was it she wanted from him? At that moment, to Clara, he appeared arrogant and self-sufficient. He felt no need to bow and scrape before her because he did not care if her father owned five acres or five thousand.

'Yes, I found the boy,' he eventually said.

'Mr Rennie, did you see the man or men who killed him?'

So that was it, out in the open at last.

'Who sent you?' he asked sharply and her colour deepened suddenly, sending a flush all the way down to the neck of her blouse.

'Nobody sends me anywhere, Mr Rennie.'

'But it seems to me that you already know the answers to all these questions you're asking me. So what exactly are you here for?'

Clara took a firm rein on her temper, checking quickly the impulse to tell this man what she thought of his high and mighty attitude towards someone in her position. Her next words were spoken slowly and deliberately so that there would be no mistakes.

'I just want to tell you that keeping out of trouble is smart. We'll all be happier if your memory continues to fail you. Good morning.'

'Miss Rutherford,' Rennie said coldly, catching her none too gently by the elbow and wheeling her to face him. 'What exactly am I to keep quiet about? Let's get our story straight shall we, for the sheriff's benefit.' She flicked his hand off her arm and answered in a tone of angry indignation.

'You know damned well what I'm talking about. Didn't you chase my man up the slope when you saw him drop Corey? Didn't he just get away in time?'

So, he'd been that close.

'Yes, ma'am,' he said softly. 'I climbed that slope.'

'My man's been in a sweat ever since. If it hadn't been for . . . well, you're still alive, aren't you? We waited to see if you would talk.'

'What kept you from seeing to me as well as Corey?' he asked her but she only smiled. 'If it hadn't been for what?' he asked her again. She had the upper hand now. There was confusion in his arrogance and her smile became a sneer.

'You're a man of intelligence. I guessed that the minute you turned your back on me. Keep quiet, Rennie. You saw the boy. You know what can happen to a man on a dark night, on a deserted stretch of road. Keep quiet,' she repeated, leaning a little closer to him, till he caught the scent of her perfume as it turned stale in the heat, a scent that reminded him of gardenias, 'and you might get another medal for bravery.'

She paused, going over what she had said, wondering if she had missed anything. For a moment she seemed unaware that he had turned quite pale under his tan and that the confusion in his eyes was wavering, hardening into something else.

She stepped up lightly into the saddle, with a little bounce of returning good humour. Her eyes travelled in a slow circle around the confines of the small, beautiful valley. In the distance the slopes were faintly mauve, undulating lazily in the heat. She turned, remembering something.

'I hope you remember what happened to you the last time you ran to the authorities without stopping to think of the consequences. The results for you were rather painful, I think.'

Her parting shot left Rennie completely stunned. He watched her neat little figure leave his yard and cut across to the road and his gaze hardened suddenly into angry disbelief. How could she know the truth? Who was it who had saved him from being killed for seeing Corey's killer? He dared not think of any such possibility, tried to calm a sudden flurry of panic inside him as he finished buttoning and tucking in his shirt. She had given him some food for thought. A three-course meal, as it turned out.

CHAPTER FOUR

Sam Cutter put down his tools for a minute to draw himself a dipper of water, drank it all and poured the second helping over his head, mopped the drops from his face with his shirt-tail and wondered, for probably the hundredth time that day, when this unusual heat would relent. Summer was always hot but this heat felt like it was coming straight up out of hell's mouth. There was no cooling breeze, no relieving shower of rain in the night to settle the dust like they usually had. If it didn't slacken soon everything would be as charred as the old barn. Work was progressing on the new one though, despite the heat and with the help of most of his immediate neighbours. The frame and three sides were already done.

Sam had opted for this measure, of raising the barn gradually over a period of a week or more rather than the traditional one-day barn raising. These people needed the reassurance that help was close to hand if need be and working daily, a few hours at a time had drawn the settlers closer together. Sam had learned that tactic from an old army captain of his. He turned from admiring the handsome skeleton of his new barn to see the man himself come walking into the front yard, leading his horse. Sam stole a glance at the men working on the barn. They had been talking about Jim Rennie today and what they had been saying was not very

31

complimentary, though they had the good sense not to say it in Sam's presence. Everybody knew too well that they were old friends and that Sam would defend Rennie to the last.

'It's too damn hot to be walkin', Jim,' Sam said with a shake of the head, reaching to take Rennie's hand.

'I think better when I walk,' he said and his eyes scanned the naked barn structure. 'Coming along fine,' he smiled, but Sam had already noted the worry, deep-seated in his eyes.

'What's wrong?' he asked.

'I might have seen something that day, at the bridge. I'm going there to look. Can I borrow Andrew?'

'All right,' Sam said slowly. 'Wouldn't it be better maybe if I came?'

'I need someone in better shape than you, Sam,' Rennie said with a little half-smile, one eye squinted slightly against the fierce sun.

'To do what?' Sam asked but Rennie could only give a little shrug, not sure how to explain the feeling he had of something he had missed that day, of something overlooked by the riverside. He felt like a man about to go digging around after something that he would just as soon have left alone.

'Well, Andy's just gettin' underfoot today anyway. I'll go get him.'

Sam walked away and Rennie took off his hat and ran a hand through his sweat-damp hair. As he resettled his hat and walked to the well for a dipper of water, he saw the men begin to leave their work and drift towards him. He drank thirstily, soaked his handkerchief in some of the water and pressed it to his neck and throat, enjoying the momentary coolness, and tensed himself for a little unpleasantness. The men formed a loose, unhurried circle about him and with deliberate slowness Rennie hung up the water ladle and started to walk away.

'Well here he is, boys,' a loud, unpleasant voice halted him, 'the man who didn't see anything.'

Tom Colton lived in the settlement closest to Sam on the western side. He was also Sam's biggest neighbour physically, being all of six foot four and about the same in breadth. He was a man who would not stand to be pushed around for long and Rutherford had not neglected Colton on account of his size or his shortness of temper. He had been pushed and goaded as much as the other settlers.

'Maybe he needs eyeglasses,' somebody else suggested and a ripple of harsh laughter went around the circle.

'Or maybe he just needs persuadin',' Colton said loudly and Rennie met his eye. It was nothing more or less than a challenge. Rennie's little voice warned him to back down from this confrontation, that Colton was not worth fighting and anyway Rennie knew his own limitations when it came to brawling. Yet he found himself angrily squashing the voice and heard himself say, in a tone unnaturally harsh to his own ears, 'Anytime you want to chance your luck, Colton.'

After a brief, charged silence, with no reply from Colton, he turned again to leave, but the ring of men around him tightened up suddenly and he no longer had any choice. Forced back into the centre, his eyes hardening to the colour of cold slate, he addressed Colton.

'You chancing your luck now?'

'Luck wouldn't have anything to do it,' the big man grated and Rennie's eyes jerked towards the close press of men.

'Just what kind of odds are you offering me here?' he asked and Colton laughed.

'You think I can't handle you on my own, Rennie?'

'You're not going to handle anybody, Tom.' It was Sam, come back from fetching Andrew. He had heard most of what had been said, but was not prepared to see bloodshed in his yard. Not Jim Rennie's blood anyway.

'Andrew's just comin', Jim,' he said evenly, lifting an eyebrow at Rennie's flushed, angry face. 'And I see you're all getting acquainted.'

'No thanks, Sam,' Colton said fiercely. 'I don't want to know anything with its belly that close to the ground.'

He threw one last bitter, venomous look at Rennie and then with a nod to the other men, turned and went back to work on the barn. Rennie unclenched the fist he was unaware he had made. His palm was crawling with sweat.

'You took your sweet time coming back,' he complained.

'Oh, I don't know. Could've bin an interestin' contest, don't you think?'

'No,' Rennie said with a rueful smile. 'I think your neighbours all need locking up.'

'Tom Colton isn't a violent man, Jim. None of them is, but they feel threatened.' Sam's face was suddenly sober. 'I guess you got yourself caught in the middle.'

Rennie looked at the busy workers on the barn and wondered privately when he was ever anything else.

'Hello, Mr Rennie,' a familiar voice said quite close to his ear and he had to struggle to look calm as he turned. 'How are you?' Eve Cutter asked him. She looked cool in a cotton dress that was almost, but not quite, the same shade as her eyes.

'I'm ... well, thank you,' he said politely, his hand automatically rising to remove his hat.

'Did you ask him yet?' she said to her father. Sam smiled but looked uncomfortable.

'No, honey, not yet but—'

'We want you to come here on Saturday,' she said to Rennie. 'We're having a party with music and food and dancing and all.'

Rennie smiled uncertainly at her and glanced at the people who had recently formed an angry cordon around him.

'It's kind of you to ask me but I don't think. . . .'

'But you've got to come. All the folks who helped put out the fire and everybody helping on the new barn are invited and that includes you.'

Rennie pretended to give it some thought, wondering how best to phrase it without offending her.

'I know what they're saying about you, about what you saw or didn't see at Sandy Creek,' Eve said, reading his thoughts.

'Then you must know that it would only cause trouble if I came,' he said with a slow shake of the head.

'But it isn't true, is it? You didn't see anyone?'

'No, I didn't.'

'Then don't you think it would be wrong to stay away? Don't you think that would be like saying you did see something?'

She had him there. He looked helplessly at Sam, whose tongue was poked way inside his cheek.

'Just the same. . . .' He shook his head again.

'Well, another time, maybe.' She sounded disappointed. She would have liked to see Rennie laughing and enjoying himself, dancing maybe. He would, she thought, cut a fine figure dancing, for Rennie's slightly jaded good looks were not to be matched, in her opinion.

'Maybe you'll change your mind,' she added hopefully and she offered him her hand. Rennie took it and held it a minute longer than was necessary and shook his head again, with a puzzled, rather sad expression on his face. The idea that he might never come closer to Eve Cutter than a brief, chaperoned conversation in her father's yard, than a polite shaking of hands, filled him with despair. As she turned to leave, he could not tear his eyes away till the house door had swung gently shut on the blue cotton dress. He turned and Sam was watching him with a thoughtful expression.

'What?' Rennie asked.

'I didn't say a thing.'

'What are you looking at me like that for?'

Sam said nothing. He rocked back on his heels, his lower lip shoved out expressively.

'She's too young for me, Sam,' he said at last.

'You mind if I say something personal, Captain?' Rennie inclined his head for some worldly, older man homily, watching as Andrew came walking towards them leading his pony.

'You,' Sam said under his breath, 'are full of horseshit,' and before Rennie could frame a suitable reply, Sam had walked away, riffling his son's hair as he passed.

'Hi, Jim,' the boy greeted him. 'Are you coming to the party on Saturday?'

'Probably not, Andy.'

'Oh. That's too bad. Mom's already bakin' stuff for it. She said she sure was glad somebody was gettin' me out of her hair,' and Jim joined in the boy's uncomplicated laughter as they walked at first up towards the bridge trail and then mounted up and began riding towards Sandy Creek.

'Aren't we goin' to your place, Jim,' the boy asked.

'No, Andy. I need you to help me find something.'

CHAPTER FIVE

The boy rode with him to Sandy Creek, mystified but prepared to do whatever was asked of him. They left the trail above the creek and walked along the edge of the drop until they were directly above the place where Corey had been found.

'Somewhere between here and the river,' Rennie said, pointing down to a tree and a low branch that had concealed the body, 'there's a piece of shiny metal. I don't know what it is, Andrew, I just glimpsed it out of the corner of my eye that day. I didn't remember about it till a little while ago,' he said, without bothering to explain to the boy the train of thought that had led him here, partly due to Clara's talk of medals, partly something much more disturbing. Andrew nodded as he looked down the slope.

'You don't know just where, like top or bottom or—'

'I climbed up here Andrew, the day I found the body. All I recall is something bright, catching my eye.'

Andrew refused to be dismayed by the vague outline of these facts. He grinned and shrugged.

'I better get started then.'

Rennie caught his arm before he went down the slope the hard way. 'It's easier to go back along the trail and down to the bridge. Work your way up from the bank there and I'll work down from here.'

Andrew did as he was asked, while Rennie began the downward search, sliding down on his rump and parting the grass and ferns with both hands. He had reached the halfway point and was leaning back on his elbows, his heels dug into the soft ground to prevent his sliding down, when Andrew, still close to the riverbank, gave a shout of triumph. He clambered up to Rennie, holding his prize in his fist.

'What you got there, Andrew?' Rennie asked, holding out his hand. It was a cross, a cheap, gilt thing, badly finished and dangling on the end of a strong chain. The chain was broken.

'It wasn't amongst the grasss, Jim.' Andrew told him breathlessly. 'Do you know where it was?'

Rennie shook his head, trying to remember where he had seen it before.

'It was hanging on a branch down there, almost in the water. If it hadn't snagged on that tree it would have been swept away.' Just like Corey, Rennie thought, clenching the cross in his fist till its jagged corner bit into his palm. A mental picture flashed briefly in front of his eyes of a man on a ridge, holding a rifle, looking down on the Cutter place, his shirt open at the throat and his cheap metal cross lying on his breast. Except that now he was able to add a face to the rest of the man. Andrew knew something had changed, knew by the look on Rennie's face. His own young face became troubled too.

'What is it, Jim? Is it somethin' bad?' he asked and after a long time Rennie looked up at him as if just seeing him for the first time. He saw that his own mood had affected the boy and felt annoyed with himself.

'I don't know, Andy,' he said softly, squeezing the boy's shoulder.

'What are you going to do?'

Rennie sat back on the grass, his elbows on his knees,

staring down at the riverbank.

'You've been a big help, Andy. But I need to ask another favour,'

'Sure,' the boy said readily.

'I have to go away for a couple of days, to Donahue. Will you tell your dad where I've gone and ask him if he would keep an eye on the stock for me?'

'I can do that.'

'So long as you tell your dad first. And Andy, I don't want you to tell anyone about what we found today, not just yet, not till I know what it means. All right?'

'Not if you don't want me to,' the boy said, feeling a little bit important to have Jim Rennie trust him like that.

'Time I was getting you home,' Rennie said, and they both climbed back to the top and walked to where the horses waited. He rode with the boy to the ridge above his home and waited till he was right in the yard before turning for home.

Back at Creeback he packed some food in the saddle-bags, filled a canteen with water and made sure the mare and foal had enough feed and water to last them till evening. He knew that Sam would not let the boy come alone. They would probably both come to Creeback to see that everything was all right for him.

As he packed his extra gear his face was set in an expression of raw misery. He pulled a strap a little too smartly and the buckskin pulled away from him, startled by his unaccustomed heavy-handedness. Then he rode up the trail once again to Ravine Crossing Bridge. On the other side he turned left and followed the road that skirted the edge of the ravine for almost four miles. The road then cut away northwards and after a further half-mile he came to a white house, much older than the houses of the settlers, white painted, two-storeyed, with a long, covered front porch. The house had a large orchard at the back, the fragrant scent of apples carrying to Rennie as he dismounted and led the buckskin to a tethering rail to one side of the front porch. It was then that he noticed the little painted sign on the house that said 'Appletrees'.

He noticed that there were a few buggies, one wagon and half a dozen horses at the side of the house. There were two trees here, giving them plenty of shade. The front door was wide open. He could hear the murmur of voices and the clink of crockery.

He took off his hat and slapped the dust from his clothes before stepping up to the porch and entering the cool, dark shade of the front hallway. There were about twenty people here and in the front parlour, taking tea, coffee and sherry wine, all wearing black and speaking in low, hushed, respectful tones. They had come, like Rennie, to pay their respects to the mother of Ben Corey. No one seemed to notice him or pay him any mind as he moved through the room in search of Mrs Corey. He felt that he would know her when he saw her. He returned to the hallway and noticed that one door was closed and with a glance at the mourners standing nearby, turned the handle and went inside.

The coffin was in here, standing on a trestle, with one or two chairs around it and within it the boy. He lay with arms folded, wearing his best suit and a clean white shirt, his hair lifelessly slicked down. Rennie rested a hand on the edge of the coffin and stood motionless beside him for almost five minutes, going over in his mind the moment of finding him and all that had followed it. He could not help thinking that this fairly anonymous young man held a vital key to something important.

'Did you know my son?' a voice asked him from the shadows in a corner of the room and Rennie gave a little start. The woman who spoke moved towards him. She wore a black

40

silk gown that stirred like dead leaves as she walked. She looked keenly at Rennie for a long time, trying to place him, and then sat down on one of the chairs by the coffin. The thin light from a window with drawn blinds showed a face exhausted with grief.

'I didn't know him well, ma'am. But it was me who found him by Sandy Creek.'

Her scrutiny became intense and she pointed to a chair opposite, indicating with a movement of her hand that he should sit.

'Your name is Rennie?' He nodded. 'They say you saw my son's killer and that you refused to tell the sheriff who it was,' she said bluntly.

He studied her face for a moment before answering. She was a woman of fifty perhaps, her hair, thin and almost completely grey, was dressed in braids wound in a crown about her head. Her nose was strong, her eyes so bloodshot with grief it was impossible to tell their colour. She was a woman whose whole life had been devoted to hard work, duty to her husband and her church and the care of her home. All of these things she had done to the very best of her ability but now as she kept vigil at the coffin of her only son she wondered if she had failed him somehow, not been as loving and caring to him as she might have been. Her guilt was an ugly pain at the pit of her stomach and everyone's good wishes and condolences only made it worse. She wanted this day to be over, so that she could have time to think.

'Ma'am, I didn't see anyone that day. I swear that to you,' Rennie said quietly. She thought about that for a minute then nodded, her eyes searching his face, which seemed as tired and drawn as her own, for the answers to questions that she did not even know how to begin to ask. The name of her son's killer was not one of them. That was something she would leave to others.

41

'I think I believe you. You seem like a decent young man. Did you come for the funeral? We won't be burying him until this evening. The minister can't come till then.' She turned her head away for a moment to look towards the window, listening as a carriage drew up. One of her three brothers had not yet arrived and she was anxious that he should come in time.

'I just wanted to pay my respects, ma'am. I'm on my way to Donahue on business.'

She stood up and held out her hand to him and he took it in both of his, his heart unbearably heavy for her.

'I do thank you for coming, Mr Rennie,' she said gently.

'I was just thinking what my own mother would have felt, if someone had brought news of my death to her door. I can't bear to think on it.'

'Your mother is still living?'

'Yes, ma'am, in Boston. Both of my parents are still there.'

'But you haven't seen her in some time?'

'No.' Rennie shook his head. 'But there isn't a day goes by when I don't think about them both. I'm afraid it's a great failing we sons have, that we can never show our parents how we feel about them.'

It was not what she had expected to hear but his words were hugely comforting to her and her tears suddenly ran unchecked. Rennie, looking distinctly unhappy, struggled for something comforting to say to her but for the first time in a week she felt a slight easing of her grief and she tried a frail smile.

'Your mother knows how you feel, Mr Rennie, I promise you. Now, will you stay with him for a moment?' she asked him. 'There's something I have to do.'

When she was gone he reached into his shirt and took out the cross and chain, held it in his hand and let it dangle on the chest of the dead man.

'Is this what you died for, Corey?' he asked. He slipped the metal into the coffin, under the small of the boy's back where he thought it would remain unnoticed and took his hand away just as Mrs Corey returned with a bottle of beer and a package of food for him.

'Something for your journey,' she said and he recognized a familiar tone in her voice for he had heard it often enough from his own mother. He gave a rueful smile.

'What?' she asked.

'For a minute there you sounded just like my own mother. She would wait at the front door when we left the house to make sure we wrapped up warm, and when we came home she was there to see if we needed food or drink or just someone to talk to.'

'Well,' Mrs Corey managed after swallowing a lump the size of a turnip in her throat, 'that's what we mothers do best. We look after our children as long as we can and then they leave us, one way or another.'

Rennie turned to leave, then paused.

'Ma'am, I've been trying to recall where your son worked in town.'

'He was at the bank for a while, but for the last year he worked in Donahue. In the telegraph office.'

CHAPTER SIX

Two nights later he returned, walking the last hundred yards into town. Donahue had been busy and bustling and dirty compared to Alexander and as he stopped to look along the quiet, tree-lined main street, with soft lamps burning on porches and behind curtained windows, he realized why he liked this little town. With its mostly white-painted houses and occasional Dutch roof, and here and there a splash of red tile, it seemed almost colonial, almost like New England. He tried the sheriff's door and found it locked, turned and saw Doctor Garson on his front porch and crossed the street to him, to ask him where Cass was.

'He was called out to some trouble on settlers' land,' the doctor told him. 'You look done in. Have you been riding hard?'

'I've been to Donahue on business. Just got back.'

'Care to let me buy you a drink?'

'I don't feel very sociable, Doctor,' Rennie admitted, 'but I'm thirsty all right.'

In Fontaine's saloon all was quiet. There was a card game going on in one corner, otherwise the place was deserted. Garson called up two beers and Rennie disposed of his eagerly, feeling the cold beer wash down the silted dust in his throat. That had been one long, hard ride, with no joy at

44

either end of it. He looked up at the mirror over the bar, the owner's pride and joy, for it had hung there, untouched, for twelve years. It let him see the dredging tiredness in his face and the ingrained frown that had been there since he and Andrew went to Sandy Creek. And it let him see the card players behind him. They had dropped their game and were moving loosely towards him.

'Well, if it isn't the captain,' the tall one said. He was thin, blond, wearing clean, dark, freshly pressed clothes. The other two were equally familiar. A dark little gypsy of a man called Gus, who hadn't shaved in four days, wore an earring and had an odd scar under one eye, almost like the imprint of a small boot heel. And then there was the other one, the cause of Rennie's long, hot ride.

He looked enough like Rennie for the puzzled doctor to know that they were brothers, the same dark hair, similar blue eyes, though the other man was thinner and had a hungry, questioning look. It was the look of a man never satisfied with what life had on offer. Steven was always looking over the next hill and around the next corner for that one, big opportunity.

'Good old Captain Rennie,' Gus said with great good humour, but Rennie's eyes were locked with his brother's.

'A thousand miles I put between us and it isn't enough.' His voice was cold with hatred and anger.

Steven Rennie watched with alarm the slightly crazy light in his brother's eyes. He had frequently wondered what Jim's reaction would be if they ever met again, and now he knew.

'It's not the way you think,' he tried soothingly. 'I didn't follow you . . . let's go talk somewhere.'

He reached out for Rennie's arm and unwittingly triggered off the explosion that had been threatening inside Jim for two days. He struck out with a straight right fist and Steven, never seeing the blow coming, took the impact directly on the right cheekbone. He staggered and went down in a tangle of chairs and flying glass. The poker chips were scattered like hard confetti and a welter of blood from his mouth and nose spattered the wreckage. Rennie waded through it to get to his brother. Garson tried to stop him but the tall man in the clean, good quality clothes restrained him with a hand on his arm.

'Leave it alone, Doc,' he cautioned.

Steven stood up, ready to fight, casting around wildly for an area of clear space where he could hold his ground, but his extravagant fall had overturned and tilted the tables and chairs all around him and he found himself stumbling over them, backing himself into a corner.

'Let's go outside if you want to fight,' he shouted at a savage-faced Rennie.

But Jim had done all the fighting he cared to do. He strode on past Steven, out through the door and went quickly across the street to the doctor's office, where he had tethered the buckskin. Garson hurried after him and caught up just as Rennie was slackening the horse's tether. They didn't speak as they faced one another. Garson was a little stunned by what he had just seen.

'Well, that was quite a reunion,' the doctor observed. 'That was your brother, wasn't it, Jim?'

Rennie said nothing. Rage tore at his insides.

'Everybody's talking about it.'

'Everybody?' Rennie asked bleakly.

'Whole town. The way Cass is telling it, you had a damned good reason for not saying what you saw on the bridge.'

'Doctor, I didn't see anything,' Rennie repeated. It was beginning to sound lame even to his own ears.

'You protected him once before though, didn't you?' Garson probed, without malice, just wanting to get at the truth.

Rennie, his head bent as he struggled to loosen the tightly

cinched rein, looked up at the doctor. 'What?' he asked huskily.

'Sam told me what happened with your brother at Fort Macauley.'

'What did he tell you?'

'That you were cashiered from the army for harbouring a man who stole the payroll, for letting that man escape from the fort, and for concealing the money in your quarters to put suspicion on yourself while he escaped.'

And the whole black, ugly nightmare of that long night at the fort surfaced again and Rennie let the reins hang loose. His shoulders drooped with sudden tiredness and he turned and climbed onto the doctor's porch and sat heavily on one of the chairs that faced the street. The doctor sat beside him, hunching forward with his elbows on his knees, while Rennie thought about what had happened at the fort, the night his brother so casually put an end to his orderly life.

'That isn't what happened,' he said and he told the doctor how it had really been at Fort Macaulay.

Rennie had known when they had arrived that they were up to no good and he was right. They, Steven, Kelly and Gus, had come to the fort for one reason only, to steal the payroll, and Steven was stupid enough to think that once they had stolen it, Jim Rennie would help them get away. But Rennie's men had closed the fort up like a fist and had started searching for them in every corner, except one. The thieves were hiding in Jim's own quarters and when they realized that he intended to turn them in they beat and roped him, forged a pass for themselves and walked out through the front gate with the money. But word got out that one of the thieves was Captain Rennie's brother and that the whole robbery had been stage-managed, the search of the camp a distraction and the beating he took a sham. He had found himself up in front of a general court and suddenly he was a civilian. But he knew he was lucky not to be in prison and that his commanding officer had had a hand in that, had been unable to stop the juggernaut of the army disciplinarians, but knowing there was no real truth in the allegations, had managed stop them from crushing a good officer.

'After what Steven did to me, I expected him to give me a wide berth. Instead of which he's here and now it's starting all over again,' Jim said, shaking his head as he looked down at his bruised and bleeding hand. He gave a cavernous sigh. 'I wondered what I would feel if I ever saw him again.'

'I thought you were remarkably restrained,' the doctor said, fiercely angry on Rennie's behalf now that he knew the whole story.

'I wanted to beat him senseless and then shoot him in the heart,' Rennie admitted with slightly raised eyebrows and a little nod. That would have assuaged some of the black grief and anger he had been nursing since the fort. 'But I think Cass would have put a rope round my neck faster than you can say homesteader.'

'If Cass knew the story, what you've told me tonight. . . .'

'No, Doctor,' he responded savagely. 'I thought the law and the proper authorities would help me at Fort Macaulay. I put my trust in them and they hung me out to dry. No. I'm handling this one on my own.'

CHAPTER SEVEN

Jim went directly to Sam Cutter's place and just as he reached the front of the house, the door opened and Sam stepped out. He was startled by Rennie's presence and came quickly forward. There was a movement behind him.

'Evening, Jim,' said Cass, appearing momentarily in the yellow oblong of the door before crossing the porch to stand on the single step looking down at Rennie, who was still in the yard. 'Finally got back did you? We was all beginnin' to think you'd gone for good.'

'Where were you, Jim? Is anything wrong?' Sam asked.

'My bank is in Donahue, Sam, you know that,' Jim lied fluently and Sam gave a lying nod of agreement back.

'We've had bad trouble while you were away. Fire at the Harrison place last night, two people hurt. And another one at the Powells' tonight. Both families are leaving in the morning.'

'Did you catch them this time, Cass?' Rennie asked the sheriff deliberately and Cass stepped down into the yard, his big jaw jutting under the strain of clenched muscles.

'Come on, Rennie,' he said tightly. 'What game is this you're playin' now?'

Rennie blinked, felt eyes strike him, Sam, Frances, Eve and a flinty, unfriendly stare from Cass.

'How come you're always these people's friend right after there's trouble?'

'That's not fair, Cass,' Frances admonished him.

'But all the time you're bein' friendly and lendin' a good old helpin' hand, when it suits you, all the time you're bein' even more chummy with Rutherford.'

'I wish you'd start proving some of this, Cass,' Rennie said mildly.

'I've got a witness,' Cass said with satisfaction, 'who saw Clara Rutherford visiting with you two days ago. Right after that you disappeared to . . . your bank, did you say? I don't know what that tells Sam here but I know what it tells me. People around here think you sit on the fence, Rennie, but you're the best damned leapfrog expert I ever saw. Mister, you're nobody's friend but your own.' He took a step as if to walk away but then stopped, a lazy smile on his face failing to hide the disgust in his eyes. 'I just about bought that story of yours too, about you not seeing anybody. Just goes to show how wrong a body can be,' and he looked meaningfully at Sam.

'What do you want from me, Cass,' Rennie asked. 'Blood?'

'No, I don't want your blood, Captain. There'll be plenty others lookin' for it and with a better right to it than me.'

He nodded to Sam and the two women and quickly fetched his horse, was gone in a minute, riding hard up to the bridge road. Jim Rennie released a tense, overlong breath and turned to find Sam's eyes on him.

'You've made an enemy,' Sam told him flatly.

'Only one? Can I talk to you, alone?' and he glanced at Frances, whose face was blank with puzzlement and at Eve, who looked as if she had already heard more than she cared to. Sam took his arm and steered him into the house, into the kitchen and firmly closed the door on the two surprised women.

50

'All right now, what is all this about your bank and Clara Rutherford visiting you? Jim, the whole county thinks you're in Rutherford's pay.'

'I can't be responsible for the whole county. I came here tonight to square things with you,' Rennie said and he sat down at the kitchen table. Sam sat down opposite, shaking his head.

'There's nothing to square. I mean you couldn't have known Steven was here. You would have had that look on your face before this. Just exactly what did you do to the bastard when you saw him?'

Rennie spread his hand on the table, displaying the burst and swollen knuckles, the whole thing set off nicely with a ring of crusted blood.

'Here, let me see that.' Sam pulled the hand towards him and turned it this way and that, testing the small bones for any breakage.

'I take it he's working for Rutherford,' Jim said, trying to draw his hand away from Sam's ungentle ministrations and failing. Sam got up to fetch a bottle from a cupboard which, when uncorked, filled the room with the smell of iodine.

'This'll hurt like hell,' Sam assured him and using a long cotton swab, dabbed at the worst areas. Rennie licked a drop of cold sweat from his lip and gave a relieved grunt when Sam was all done.

'Yes, he's at Rutherford's. Cass saw him yesterday when he went out to ask a few questions. He saw the resemblance, asked him who he was. Now everybody thinks you've bin spyin' on us somehow, takin' information back to Rutherford. If they knew the truth about you two, they'd have to think again, wouldn't they?'

Rennie narrowed his eyes, recalling how the 'truth' had helped him in the face of a general court.

'Which truth do you think they'd believe, Sam? What they

51

charged me with at my trial or what really happened?'

'Anyway, I told Doctor Garson, a little anyhow. I couldn't let him think you were involved with Steven and his cronies.'

'I met him tonight.' Rennie suddenly remembered the version of events the doctor had told and wondered where that had come from, certainly not Sam. But he had so many other things to think about that the thought went to the back of his mind, where it would stay for some time.

'Tomorrow, I'm going to Rutherford's to see Steven and his friends. I mean to make them move on.'

Sam rested a cheek on his knuckles and raised one sceptical eyebrow.

'I can't stand the suspense. How?'

'Did you know that there's a US marshal in Donahue? Well, I went to see him. He brought me up to date on Steven's activities since I saw him last. I'm sure Cass would be very interested to hear all about it. And Clara Rutherford did visit me. She warned me against telling anyone who I saw that day on the bridge.'

'But you didn't see anyone.'

'We both know that, but Clara doesn't. The killer saw me and thought I saw him and reported back to her. They were going to kill me too, Sam,' he said soberly, 'but Steven seems to have told her that I would keep my mouth shut. And of course, I didn't tell anybody what I saw because I didn't see anything. She misinterpreted my actions and seems to think I'm just a coward or a fool or both.'

'Somebody else who's going to have to think again,' Sam said quietly.

'But after Clara left that morning, I remembered seeing something at the river bank. That's when I came for Andrew. Did he tell you what we found?'

'Wild horses wouldn't drag it out of him. Not even when I promised him a liquorice stick and a quarter,' Sam said with a wry grin.

'We found a little souvenir from the killer, a cheap metal cross. It belongs to Kelly. I think some whore gave it to him.'

'Where is it now?'

'Someplace safe. Maybe it would be better if you don't know where. But it's evidence that'll hang him, unless he does what I want.'

Sam saw the danger in what his friend intended to do and so did Rennie and in silence for a moment they both contemplated what might happen.

'Even if they go, I don't think the violence will stop,' Rennie said with a shrug. 'At best it'll give you a breathing space.'

'If it gives Rutherford a bloody nose for once I'll be grateful,' Sam smiled. Rennie got up, ready to leave.

'I'll ride with you a little ways, for company,' Sam offered but Rennie shook his head.

'Thanks anyway. I'll see you tomorrow.'

When the door had closed behind him, Frances, who had been eavesdropping at the door that led to the front parlour, came in and sat down opposite her husband. She lifted the little iodine bottle and gave Sam a look of mild enquiry in response to which he blew all the air out through his cheeks and shook his head.

'Think our boy is about to put his head in the lion's den, Fran.'

Rennie stood for a moment on the porch, letting the brave face of determination he had put on for Sam dissolve into the dull, tired look that had been there all the time. He felt as if his world was falling to pieces and he was not really sure he had the energy to hold it together. In the shadows, Eve stood watching him and now she came forward a little and spoke to him softly.

'Will you stay and talk for a minute?'

He turned with a little jump of surprise, his heart constricting as it always did when he saw her. She tilted her head and the light from the kitchen fell on her face. His face was masked as usual with a look of polite enquiry. It no longer fooled her. She had seen the mask slip down tonight and the jaded, unhappy look underneath made her sick at her heart. He lifted his hand to remove the hat he had not taken off in the house and she saw the battered knuckles.

'Oh, Jim,' she cried and reached for the hand, looking down at it with difficulty in the poor light. Holding his wrist she led him nearer the porch light and examined it more closely. She bound it up with her handkerchief and Rennie let her carry on, experiencing a slight but pleasurable increase in blood pressure as she held his fingers.

'What happened?' she asked, her head bowed.

'I got into a fight,' he answered huskily as her hair brushed his face. She looked up sharply.

'You did, Mr Rennie?' she said with a bewildered half-smile. 'Who with?'

'With my brother.' He slipped his hand out of her grasp.

'So it's true then, what Cass told us. What did he do to deserve that?' She gave him a long, considering look and found herself being considered in return.

'I was in the army once,' he told her drily. 'My brother saw to it I got out of the army in a hurry. I didn't hit him because of that. I hit him because he followed me here and has already succeeded in turning my life inside out again. I intend to see to it that he moves on.'

'What are you going to do?' she asked him, not liking this new look of impacted anger. 'Whatever it is,' she said and she placed a hand on each of his shoulders, 'you'll be careful.'

For once Rennie did not stop to think, to weigh the pros and cons. He kissed her, with some passion, forcing her suddenly back against the wall of the house, though holding her there with great gentleness.

He had wanted to kiss her since the day and hour he met her, but his mistake was in thinking that one kiss would satisfy or at lease ease his longing for her. It did not. The brief, fiery embrace left Rennie with a dry mouth and the unpleasant sensation that all his clothes were too tight.

When he disengaged, drawing his head back and sliding his hands down the warm inward slope of her back and away from her, he realized how hard he was breathing. Eve's eyes were wide, her lips half open as she reluctantly let him go, her hands slipping down his arms, holding the edges of his hands for a moment before she stepped back. They continued to look at one another for a long minute in silence, both a little shocked by the tension they had managed to create. He replaced his hat, looking at her in that same, sober thoughtful way as he turned to leave.

Eve folded her arms and watched him walk to his horse and listened until he was out of earshot. She had been kissed before but no one had ever made her feel that way and nobody else ever would. She loved him and at least now she knew that he felt pretty much the same. And now he was probably going to go and get himself killed, just when they were starting to get somewhere.

'Story of my life,' she said aloud to the darkness.

CHAPTER EIGHT

The heat was settling for the night when Rennie returned and the valley was deathly still. For a minute he leaned against the corral, his hat on the back of his head, eyes tenderly scanning the creamy, moonlit silhouette of his land. The place had a strange quality about it tonight, as if it were that dead area at the eye of a hurricane. Rennie had lived out a lot of years in the space of a few days and exhaustion came now, robbing him suddenly of the desire to do anything but sleep.

But old habits die hard. He stripped the buckskin and gave the old horse a good half-hour's grooming, loosening the trail dust from his rough coat and combing his mane and tail, checking and clearing his hoofs, then seeing to his supper and making sure there was plenty of fresh water. Then he spent a few minutes just leaning close to the old boy and stroking his chest and gently rubbing the criss-cross of scars on his body, which he seemed to like.

'Who did that to you, boy?' Rennie asked for the hundredth time, fingering the mesh of scar tissue on his neck and flank. The old horse whickered and rubbed his nose on Rennie's neck and the question of who had hurt and abused him remained unanswered.

Finally, his last action of the night, he turned for the barn to stow the saddle and gear and to take a look at the mare and her foal.

The barn door swung heavily shut behind him as he arranged the saddle across a low partition wall and hung up the other gear, and in the almost total darkness he crossed the floor to where a storm lantern hung on ceiling hook.

But something warned him that he was not alone, some instinct, war-bred and prairie-sharpened. He reached into his pocket for a match and lit the lantern and turned for the mare's stall, his heart accelerating suddenly with anticipation.

At the last minute he veered sharply and plunged towards his saddle and the rifle that was in the saddle boot. But they brought him down before he had gone two strides, one tackling him about the thighs and knees, another catching onto his right elbow and a third throwing himself across Rennie's back.

He came down with a jarring thud, the straw on the floor only partially absorbing the weight of three full-grown men landing on top of him. His arm was twisted around behind him and he was turned over, lying now on that trapped arm, the pain stretching his mouth briefly. With a man on every corner of his person, Rennie's struggle was soon done. He knew that it was no use and lay still finally, his breathing harsh and painful due to a knee on his breastbone.

They hoisted Rennie to his feet and dragged him closer to the storm lantern and held him there, a man on each arm. Rennie spat out a mouthful of straw and lifted his head as a familiar bulk shifted into the light in front of him. It was Tom Colton.

'You know what we're here for?' Colton asked.

'Let me go now and I'll forget this ever happened. Get off my property and nobody need ever know about it.' Rennie said with a good deal more calm than he felt.

Colton gave the suggestion some thought. He fingered his

chin and pursed his mouth and then he hit Rennie a back-handed blow that would have sent him crashing through the wall if strong hands had not been holding him. His head jerked and his mouth filled with warm, coppery blood that ran in a dark smear down his lip and chin. Rennie shook his head to clear it and regarded Colton's spadelike hands with fresh respect.

'I say again, do you know what we're here for?' Colton repeated clearly, as if to a child. Rennie was silent, but there was defiance in it and Colton was starting to get angry.

'You know who killed him, don't you.'

He could not tell them, could not let them ride into a reception of rifles and revolvers because Rutherford would not let them casually ride onto his property to take one of his men to a rope. Rennie wanted no part of a massacre.

'You see, Captain, we know that your brother works for Rutherford. We know you've bin playin' Sam Cutter for a fool all along, but you're going to give us the truth, now, tonight. You can give it to us easy, or the other way.' Colton's voice was like a rasp, his face a yellowish, sweating mask of hatred. 'Who killed the boy?'

'I didn't see anybody,' Rennie answered coldly, and truthfully. He glanced to right and left at the two brothers who held him, Hal and John Graham. They owned the poorest, meanest piece of land in the whole area and there was grimness, a determination in the way that they gripped his arms. Standing to the right and slightly behind them was Lucas Collins and he took an impulsive step forward now.

'Get on with it, Tom,' he grated.

'All right.' It was obvious that Colton's patience was all used up. 'Douse that light,' he told Collins with what seemed to Rennie like an excess of caution. As they waited for Collins to walk back to the lamp hanging by the door, Rennie launched his right foot, kicking Colton in the genitals. While

Colton doubled, unable to strangle his scream of agony,
Rennie pivoted and smashed his boot into John Graham's
shin. As he fell away, clutching at his leg, Rennie swung his
free left fist around at Hal. His knuckles ploughed into the
big farmer's jaw, sending him staggering.

Again Rennie turned for the saddle and this time he
reached it, was about to slide the rifle free when Collins
reached him. He hit Rennie with both fists, in the small of the
back, a vicious blow that had all the pent up frustration of
tonight's business behind it and it finished Rennie. He made
a sound at the back of his throat like an animal caught in a
trap and arched his back as the sickening pain blinded him
and then rocked him backwards in a dead faint.

Collins caught him as he fell and the others, who had
quickly regrouped, arrived to help lift him. They were
breathless and shocked at the speed of the whole thing,
surprised even at the way Rennie had defended himself, with
guts and spirit when they had all been led to believe Rennie
was nothing but a chicken-livered fence-sitter.

As they took up their former positions, they really had to
hold him now. Tom Colton limped around in front of him,
winded and hurting more than he cared to admit. Rennie
dragged his head up, his eyes unfocused and glassy, teeth
clenched. His back was on fire.

'One last time,' Colton's voice was strident now. 'Who
killed the boy?'

'You're not doing yourself a bit of good Colton . . . down
here in the gutter. That's how they . . . that's how they fight.
In the dark . . . in the back.'

'Who do you mean "they", Rennie?' Colton asked acidly.
'You are "they". You are our enemy. Who killed the boy?'

'I didn't see . . . I didn't see anybody.'

'Is that your answer?'

'Go home, Tom,' Rennie tried one last time, fighting

against faintness and nausea and the throb of that still excruciating back pain. But Tom Colton had come too far to go home.

He looked down at his two fists; two of the deadliest weapons he could call to any crisis. Yet he believed that this fight was not of his choosing, believed that he had been forced to come here by events beyond his control. Rennie had kin at Rutherford's and he held the key to the whole thing if he would only talk. He had to be made to talk.

'Tell us, man, for God's sake,' Lucas Collins urged him. Rennie's reply was to shift his feet, bracing himself, knowing what was to come and, in silence, looked straight into Tom Colton's eyes. The men who held him that night would remember that for a long time.

'I'm sorry,' Colton said, but his voice had hardened and he did not sound in the least sorry. 'There isn't any room for neutrals in this war.' And he struck Rennie and struck him again and when he fell they kicked him, though he felt nothing and knew nothing and was drowning in blackness when they dragged him outside.

CHAPTER NINE

Alder was one of Rutherford's cattlemen. His day was almost over and as he made his way home, shoulders slouched, hat settled comfortably on the back of his head, he took a minute to roll and light himself a long, thin cigarette. The smoke trailed from his nostrils as he continued on his way.

It was late, already dark. He had cooked his own supper out on the line where he had been working, where he would have bedded down for the night were it not for the fact that his bones had warned him of a storm on the way. Tomorrow, if the storm had not already broken, he would wangle a job in the yard. At the moment there was just a smell of it, nothing more.

He was just a mile from the ranch house now when on the trail ahead of him, wandering aimlessly, he saw a riderless buckskin horse. It stopped when it saw him and stood patiently still when he reached for the dangling rein.

'You're a good old fella. Old army pony, ain't ya?' Alder murmured and that was when he saw that he had been wrong about one thing. The horse was not riderless.

He led the buckskin up to the big house and knocked on the door, to tell them what he had found. Miss Clara herself came down the steps, wearing a blue velvet gown, jewels on her ears and wrists. Alder, unshaven and unwashed for a week, felt like a dinosaur standing next to her. She circled the horse to examine the body that had been tied over the saddle, lifting the upside down head. When she saw who it was she gave a low, husky laugh, not a ladylike laugh at all, Alder thought. He looked over her shoulder and saw that two of the men she was always with these days had followed her outside. Alder wondered, not for the first time, why Mr Rutherford would let men like that in his house, drifters, paid help with guns on their thighs.

'Take him inside,' she told Kelly and Gus and then gave a nod to Alder. 'Thanks for bringing him in. You better turn in now.'

He nodded, tweaked the brim of his hat and ambled off to the bunkhouse, wondering to himself why any woman would laugh at seeing a man who had been beaten like that man had. He found his own bunk in the dark, quiet as an Indian so as not to wake the others, and slept soundly, unaware of what he had done by bringing Jim Rennie back with him.

Kelly and Gus carried him down a long corridor to a room under the stairs and laid him, still senseless, onto a narrow bed in the corner. They went away laughing, saying aloud how much they were looking forward to telling Steven what had happened.

On the narrow bed, Jim Rennie started to surface and at first there was only pain, all down the length of him, one vast, pulsating ache that broke sweat on his face the moment he tried to move.

'Oh Christ,' he said reverently, falling back on the pillow. Eventually, the pain localized itself to his back. All other ailments fell secondary to this one, raw, nagging spot, even his swollen, blood encrusted face and his injured hand, the one Eve had so carefully bandaged for him, did not hurt so much. Strangely, her little temporary binding had survived the mauling.

After a time that might have been minutes or hours, he looked around him. It was a small, cluttered room with a slanted ceiling, filled with oddments of furniture, a bureau, washstand, four dining chairs stacked on top of one another, even a long-case grandfather clock, all loomed around him, good, heavy, expensive pieces of furniture, brought from back East.

He guessed he was in the Rutherford house. There were not many other houses in this area with spare rooms under the stairs to put unexpected guests into. He wondered, without enthusiasm, how he had come to be here. Wondering didn't help. Eventually he sat up, carefully, and swung his legs to the floor. He found that if he moved slowly the pain was bearable. He stood up, one hand on the wall for support, waiting till his heart slowed, and then moved forward to the door.

He opened it onto a long corridor that led to the main body of the house. It was not far to walk to the room where he could hear voices but Rennie's face was white as paper, his body trembling gently with the effort required to stay upright by the time he reached the half-open door.

Beyond the door and unexpectedly for Rennie, was a room that brought with a surge, memories of his mother's house in Boston. This room was softly lit with several gleaming lamps, the walls book-lined, and the lamplight gleaming on their leather bindings. Heavy red velvet draperies hung at the double windows and Turkey rugs added rich colour and texture to the floor.

Rennie felt disoriented for a moment transported back from Creeback, from Fort Macauley, from the war itself, back to civilization again, to the comfort and security of home in Boston. He almost expected the woman at the window closing the curtains against the darkness to be his mother, turning with a warm smile to greet him.

But it was Clara Rutherford who turned, her gold earrings glinting in the lamplight. Her two companions seated on the leather furniture were Kelly and Gus. They looked as odd and out of place as foxes at a tea party.

'Why, Mr Rennie, you do seem to have been in the wars,' Clara said, crossing the floor to stand before him.

'How did I get here?' he asked coldly and Clara raised an eyebrow at his tone.

'One of my men found you tied over your horse on my property. About a mile from this house, actually.'

Rennie laughed without humour at the thought of Tom Colton ordering him to be tied over his horse and then turned loose on Rutherford land. He also noted her use of the word 'my', my men, my property.

'I'm glad you find something funny after tonight, Mr Rennie,' she remarked.

'Well, I do find it funny that I seem to be talking to you all the time, Miss Rutherford. Doesn't your father give the orders around here any more?'

Now it was Clara's turn to smile.

'No,' she said quietly, 'not any more.'

Rennie's eyes turned to Kelly, who was busily helping himself to some of Tom Rutherford's brandy.

'You're not very fussy about the help you keep, are you?' he said drily and Clara laughed her low, husky laugh. As she looked at the tall blond man, he seemed to her like a shaggy-coated puma, powerful and dangerous. To Rennie he looked like a mangy, flea-ridden prairie dog but without a prairie dog's innate dignity. But Kelly was dangerous, Rennie would concede that. He had killed Ben Corey and now he stood there sipping French brandy and looking like a tame house cat.

'It's late,' Kelly said, setting the delicate little glass down on the drinks tray. 'I guess I'll turn in. You want me to put this clown back in the closet, Miss Clara?' He always called her that around company.

'No, he needs cleaning up. Why don't you all turn in,' she said with a nod that included Gus. Kelly hesitated, looking at Rennie with plain dislike and distrust. He did not like him being here. It gave him a bad feeling.

'I'll be all right,' Clara assured him, with a twinkling, knowing smile. 'I don't think Mr Rennie will do me any harm.'

With that Kelly shrugged, a 'you're the boss' shrug, and ambled out of the room, taking Gus with him.

'Why don't you sit down, Mr Rennie?'

'Why don't you have my horse brought around and I'll be on my way, Miss Rutherford.'

'Nonsense, you're my guest. I didn't ask you here, but now that you are, the least I can do is provide a little iodine for your cuts.'

Reluctantly, but partly because his curiosity was piqued, Rennie sat on a straight-backed chair while Clara brought clean water, iodine and cotton swabs. With forefinger under his chin, she tilted his head into the light and appraised his face. Once the blood was cleaned away it looked a little better but hardly pretty.

'Why did you let them do that to you?' she asked him and for once there seemed to be no malice or sarcasm in her voice.

'I don't like to be herded by a mob.'

'Let me see if I've got it straight. They asked you who killed Corey and you refused to tell them. That should make you my ally, but I get the feeling you're not.'

'I'm not anybody's ally.'

'Still, you didn't tell them,' she said thoughtfully. She was examining his hand now, the one he had punched his brother with, and the one with Eve Cutter's handkerchief around it. He pulled his hand gently away, not wanting her to touch it.

'Why are you railroading these people?' he asked her. She gave him a sharp look and then smiled to herself as she began replacing the things she had used from her surgical case. She put it away in a drawer and then brought him a little glass of her father's prized brandy.

'I need the land.' Her tone was uncompromising.

'That much I know. You must want it very badly to burn people out and kill their children for it.'

Clara didn't even feign shock at his words. Seeing that he didn't want the brandy she took it from him and drank it in one deep swallow.

'What have you offered them, financially, I mean?'

'More than any of it's worth. I've made generous compensatory offers on all sides,' she said, her face taking on a blank, hard look and he knew she was lying. He sighed and rose to his feet. For a dizzy moment he had to hold on to the back of the chair. His back hurt like hell, a million needle points stabbing him at once.

'In other words, you're running them off to get the land at rock-bottom prices.'

'Why, Mr Rennie, I don't believe I said any such thing.'

'You know I was right about you the first time, Miss Rutherford,' Rennie said with a rueful shake of the head. 'You're no lady.'

'And after all the money my father spent trying to turn me into one,' she sighed. 'But you're absolutely right. In fact I have it on good authority that I am a bastard, dyed in the wool. Come, I'll show you back to your room. You look like you ought to be lying down.'

'By the way,' Rennie said as they walked back down the long corridor, 'Where is my brother?'

'Oh,' Clara gave a small shrug. 'He had a little errand to

66

take care of for me. He'll be here before you leave in the morning.'

CHAPTER TEN

The long-case clock in the corner of the room chimed on the quarter-hour, the half-hour and the hour and Rennie heard every tick of the pendulum and every toll of the bell as that long night wore away towards the dawn. At a little after four he decided to move. He felt a little better, a little rested and there was something he needed to do.

He rose with care, trying not to aggravate those areas of his body made recently tender and moved to the door. She had not locked him in. He was a guest, she had said. He looked out and the corridor was empty. He walked its length and climbed the stairs to the first floor, avoiding the middle of the stair treads.

At the top he was faced with a battery of doors but he had already worked out that the master bedroom had to be at the end of this corridor, facing west, for a room situated here would command the best view of the ranch. And he hoped that what he was looking for would be in the master bedroom. He walked on the balls of his feet along the corridor to the single door at the western end. The handle turned easily in his hand and as soon as he stepped into the room he knew that it was empty. A light from somewhere below, on the porch maybe or in the yard reflected up onto the ceiling and showed him a big bed with a handsomely carved headboard, the clean white counterpane folded back, but no occupant. It had an unused, slightly musty smell and there was dust on the surfaces of dresser and washstand.

Rennie returned to the corridor, momentarily stumped. He leaned against the wall and then slid down into a crouch to ease his aching back. He turned his head to look back along the corridor and saw something interesting. It was a flight of stairs, the entrance recessed slightly, leading to an attic level.

Rennie climbed and found that there was only one door where the stairs ended and it was locked. Stretching, he ran fingers all around the jambs, searching for a key on a hook or nail, but instead found a bolt, which slid back easily, another just like it at the foot of the door and then he was in.

It was totally black in here and Rennie closed the door and leaned his back against it, waiting for his eyes to adjust to the intense darkness. He could hear breathing and soon he was able to distinguish the bulk of a bed against the wall facing him, not as large and grand a bed as the one in the room below but at least the man Rennie had been searching for was in it.

'You there,' a voice rasped from the darkness. 'What are you doing in here?'

Rennie moved deeper into the room until he stood by the bedside. A match flared and a lamp spread a thin yellow light across the room. Tom Rutherford fell heavily back against his pillows, as if the simple act of lighting the lamp had exhausted him. His eyes were bright and alert though and they regarded Rennie with interest.

'Did you meet up with a grizzly on your way here?'

'Four of them,' Rennie answered and Rutherford gave a gruff laugh.

'Who the devil are you anyway, creeping around my house in the dead of night?'

'My name's Jim Rennie. I come from a little place across the ravine called Creeback.'

'Creeback,' Rutherford breathed. He had seen the valley once a long time ago and had fallen for it just as hard as Rennie had done at first sight. He had almost settled there, but the valley had obvious disadvantages for an ambitious man and greed for more and bigger horizons had driven him across the chasm to this, to slow death at the hands of murderers.

'I know you now,' he said with nod and a narrowing of sharp, intelligent eyes. 'You're the one they kicked out of the army. And it's your brother whose been tearing down everything I've spent my life trying to build up, him and that little half-Cree Gus and the other one, that murdering heathen Kelly.'

'Those men are your daughter's paid help, Mr Rutherford. I'm not on anybody's payroll,' Rennie answered and then a sudden wave of dizziness left him sweating, one hand going to the small of his back.

'Are you all right, Rennie?' Rutherford asked.

'Is it all right if I sit down, sir?'

'Sure,' Rutherford said quietly, his tone and mood changing suddenly. 'Sit down, son.'

Jim sat on the edge of the bed, taking the weight off his shaking legs for a minute and then drew a long, tired breath.

'What's going on here, Mr Rutherford?'

Tom Rutherford gave a deep sigh. He had been waiting for someone to ask him that question for quite some time now.

'They've been trying to finish me,' he said grimly. 'But I'll be finished when they spade my grave, not before. All the years I've lived here I never had a second of trouble with the settlers, had all the land I needed to the east. Then my daughter came home. My wife wanted her to go to all the best schools, Europe, all that. She was always greedy, spoiled, hard-

70

hearted but she came back worse, with those three in tow. Where she met them, God alone knows, but right from the start there was trouble. I put up with it for a while then just as I was about to put a lid on it, kick them out, I had my "accident".'

Rennie had been wondering about Rutherford being out of the limelight all these months. He knew Rutherford by sight, had seen him several times in town. The man in the bed had obviously undergone a harrowing illness. His broad, usually tanned face was thin and sallow, sickly-looking, the eyes yellow and pouchy. The whole man seemed to have shrunk somehow.

'My horse threw me,' Rutherford continued. 'I broke my leg and busted some ribs. A doctor from Donahue, not Doc Garson, told me I'd damaged something inside and that I'd need to rest up a while. Next thing I knew I was in the damned attic. She's kept me shut up here ever since. She's been putting something in my food and water so that I'm too weak to move. I was just lying here a minute ago thinking that it was all over for me when you came through that door.'

Rutherford gave Rennie an enquiring look from clear eyes in a withered face and Rennie looked uncomfortable and shifted his weight on the bed. He didn't like to tell Rutherford that he had been brought to the ranch unconscious, that he had been given no choice in the matter.

'You asked me a minute ago what was going on,' Rutherford went on. 'Well, before I tell you the rest, I want to ask you the same thing. Why are you here in this house? Why do you look as if you've just lost an argument with a herd of buffalo?'

'A boy was killed at Sandy Creek. Your daughter and one or two other people thought I saw the killer. She came to my home and threatened me with a similar fate if I didn't keep quiet and from that moment I've been getting in deeper and

71

deeper, trying to get at the diseased heart of your daughter's little world.' Rennie gave Rutherford a bleak smile then leaned forward with his elbows on his knees. 'I'll be honest with you, Mr Rutherford, the men who did this to me dumped me on your land tonight because they figured it was where I belonged. I didn't come to rescue you, didn't even know that this had been done to you. But Clara talks too much and I started to realize that you just weren't around any more and I wanted to know why.'

'So you came looking. I'm grateful for that. Now at least somebody knows, though I'm not sure you'll want to help me once I tell you the rest.'

Rennie looked down at the worn carpet, clasping his two hands and knowing with a sudden certainty that this was going to be about Steven.

'For a few days, after I was hurt, I was still in my own bedroom, a fine big room overlooking the ranch. Even from my bed I could see the yard and all that goes on.'

'I know. I went there first tonight looking for you.' Rennie said with a smile and a little shrug. Rutherford paused, impressed with Rennie's perception and then continued.

'One of my boys, young fella called Forrest, came up to see me. I was still allowed visitors then. He showed me a broken girth strap and piece of spur. The strap had been cut almost in half and the broken spur was under the saddle, my saddle. At the time I didn't know the half of what was going on, didn't know what she was capable of. I sent the boy to her, God help me, to tell her to find out who'd done this to me.' Rutherford's eyes told Rennie the rest of the story. 'He left the yard that night with your brother. I saw them leave from my window. The horse brought him back sometime through the night. His foot was caught in the stirrup. He'd been dragged for miles. They didn't even recognize him at first.'

Rennie stood up tiredly and walked around the small

room, stooping to look out of the tiny window that overlooked the back area where there was a kitchen garden and a straggle of outbuildings. When he had gone to Donahue, he had found out things about his brother that he would have had difficulty explaining to his mother, but murder, downright cold-blooded killing was still a big shock.

'I didn't think he was capable of that,' he said, returning to the bed and easing down onto it again.

'I'm sorry, boy, but he's a killer.'

'He's in good company,' Rennie said, and he told Rutherford, as briefly and simply as he could about Kelly and his cheap crucifix, though not where it was hidden.

'Well, I guess that means we both have proof,' Rutherford said.

'Sir?'

'The girth strap and the spur. Forrest hid them for me, before he went to Clara. I didn't know she was involved but I wasn't a complete idiot. One day I'll use that evidence to put a rope around your brother's neck. And maybe you can do the same for Kelly.'

'Well, let's not go crossing any bridges before we get to them. Why does your daughter want to run the settlers off? I don't personally care what she does to them, but I have a friend , . . and I'm involved in it now whether I want to be or not.'

'Railroad,' Rutherford said simply. 'Coming through in two years' time, right through the entire western section of settlers' property and across the ravine near to where the bridge is now. Clara intends to own that land by then and intends to bargain with the railroad for a cattle depot, right on her own backyard.'

'Makes sense,' Rennie conceded, 'If only she didn't have to burn and kill settlers to get it. How come she knows about this before anybody else?'

'She still has a lot of friends back East.'

Rennie stared at Rutherford in earnest concentration for a minute, trying to make a connection in his brain with something the older man had just said. Then it came to him and he shut his eyes and gave a little groan at his own stupidity.

'What?' Rutherford asked.

'I think I know why Corey died now.'

'Corey, the boy you told me about?'

'His name was Ben Corey and he worked in the telegraph office.' Rennie said. 'He most likely intercepted a message that Clara thought would have alerted the settlers. She probably paid him to bring any messages straight out to the ranch, then sent Kelly back with him, to kill him. She must have sweet-talked him, made him promises.'

'You're right. She has the telegram, probably downstairs in the study somewhere. She had it in her hand the night she told me about the railroad coming through. She comes up here a lot, to tell me things that I can't do anything about.' Rutherford said with a wry smile.

'Then maybe I ought to find it. The more evidence we have, the better.'

'Son,' Rutherford said with sudden seriousness, resting a thin hand on Rennie's forearm, 'you've got to watch your back. These people she's filled my ranch with, they don't care who they hurt.'

'Never mind about me. What about you? Are you going to be all right up here?'

'You've given me something to hope for. That'll keep me going,' he said and he held out his hand to Rennie.

'I've got to leave now. But I'll get back to you as soon as I can.' Jim reached forward and turned down the lamp, speaking a last word to the shadowy figure on the pillows. 'I didn't start it, but I guess I've got to finish it.'

74

'Sure,' Rutherford said after the door had quietly shut on the man from Creeback. 'Just so long as it doesn't finish you, son.'

CHAPTER ELEVEN

Rennie descended the darkened stairway slowly, his outstretched fingers brushing the wall. One thing he knew for sure after his little talk with Rutherford was that what he had learned tonight would be for no one's ears but Sam's. The men who had waited for him in the barn would think he was lying if he told them Christmas came in December, nor was he likely to do much convincing of Cass. No, he would deal with the woman and her thugs in his own way.

He guessed that the room Rutherford called the study was the room he had gone to initially. He let himself in and closed the door behind him quietly. The fire in the grate had burned down to a dull red glow and by the light from that he found the desk on the far wall and began searching through the unlocked drawers for the telegram. It was not in any way hidden but lying on top of a pile of bills and business letters, held down by a glass paper weight. He took the flimsy paper to the fire and read it in the flickering light.

It would not have meant a thing to anyone not acquainted with the facts. There was no mention of the railroad, in fact the telegram contained only one sentence. Ravine crossing, six months. Corey must have known something. Perhaps he had been told just enough, so that he would take any message from Clara's informer straight to her and then when he had

76

outlived his usefulness, Kelly had removed him.

A footstep sounded at the door and he quickly stashed the telegram inside his shirt and hid behind the door where the shadows were deepest.

It was Clara. She locked the door behind her and, taking a taper from the fire, lit the lamp on the desk. Clara, like her mother before her, was a poor sleeper. Her remedy was work. As she sat down behind the desk to begin some late night paper work, Rennie moved slightly to watch her. He found himself admitting that she was an extremely beautiful woman. Her hair, a glossy blue-black in the lamplight, had been brushed out and then secured in a long thick plait. She wore a thin silk robe over her nightgown and through its soft folds, Rennie could plainly see the curve of her breasts and stomach and the swell of her thighs, but nothing stirred in him. It was the beauty of something carved, cold and heartlessly perfect. He could not imagine her helping to fight a fire, with a streak of dirt on her nose or serving coffee to exhausted men.

She was searching in the drawer that formerly held the telegram and Rennie, seeing that she was about to notice that it was gone, moved from the corner to the fireplace, watching how she rummaged, first in the correct drawer and then every other until she knew it was not there and knew that someone was standing by the hearth, his foot resting on the fender.

She lifted her head, pushing a loose strand of hair impatiently from her eyes. She saw without surprise that it was Rennie and that he was holding a piece of paper and she knew at once that it was her telegram. She held her breath as she watched him deliberately open and read the contents, his lips pursed thoughtfully. When he had read it he folded the paper into a long spill and held it against a burning log.

There was no point, she knew, in sacrificing her dignity and dashing towards him to snatch the already burning fragment from his hand. She had been about to destroy the

77

evidence herself tonight anyway. Nor did it matter that he had read the telegram, that he knew everything. He could, he would be dealt with. He dropped the last inch of burning paper into the fire and when he turned, she had circled the desk and was standing only a few feet away.

'With all due respect, Miss Rutherford, you are as devious as a corkscrew,' he said and she smiled.

'I'll take that as a compliment. Now, how did you know where that telegram was, Mr Rennie?'

'I didn't,' he lied 'I simply made a systematic search of the desk until I found it. Careless of you to leave a valuable piece of paper like that lying around.'

'But how,' she persisted, 'did you know of its existence? Have you been talking to my father?'

'Your father? I heard a rumour he was dead. If you would but credit me with a little intelligence, Miss Rutherford, you would see that since I knew where Corey worked it was not too difficult to work out why he died.'

Since it suited her for the moment to believe him, she nodded.

'So here you are, Mr Rennie the neutral, whom I find skulking in my study, going through my private business. That's hardly the action of an uncommitted man.'

'Well, you're the one committed me. You're the one told me who killed the boy.'

'I told—' That rocked her, hard as any punch.

'I didn't see anybody on that ridge, but you told me your man was there. It never occurred to you that I might not have seen him but you had to ride onto my place with your threats. If you'd let me alone you'd have your railroad and all the land you could possibly want.'

Clara drew a painful breath. She had not made a mistake of such proportions in years. She shrugged. Her hand went to the pocket of her robe and fingered the door key. One shout would have brought help but she had locked the door, because she had intended to open the safe. She looked at the tall man blocking her path to the door, looked at the span of his shoulders and the quiet, odd little smile on his face, almost as if he knew what she was thinking.

'So now you can pay me back for threatening you, take what you know to the sheriff.'

'I don't want revenge, Miss Rutherford. I want guarantees.'

Clara Rutherford did not like being told to do things, nor to obey rules imposed on her by others, but she was in a corner here and she thought it best, wisest, simply to listen.

'Go ahead, Mr Rennie.'

'My brother Steven,' he said and she gave him a strange, almost pitying look, as if she thought him gullible and naive where his brother was concerned. He ignored the look.

'I won't go to Cass if Steven leaves and takes his friends with him. Not just Kelly and Gus but every hired gun and paid muscle on the place. By Friday, at the latest.'

Clara wondered what he had to back up his demand. She was sure he had evidence, otherwise he would not have so carelessly burned the telegram.

'I take it you have proof of some kind?'

'Ask Kelly. Ask him if he's missing a personal item that belonged to him.'

'You mean . . . he isn't wearing that ugly Mexican cross any more. Is that it?'

'I have evidence that will implicate Kelly, Gus and my brother. But the most damning evidence now in my possession is against you. And if anything happens to me,' he finished quietly, 'the cross, everything I have goes straight to someone who can act on it. And don't assume I mean Cass.'

It was a hard ultimatum. From where Clara stood there seemed to be no alternative but to comply, or appear to.

'You bastard,' she said calmly and Rennie shook his head.

'Don't talk about my mother that way, Miss Rutherford. In any case, you might as well know. I'm not doing this for the homesteaders. I've never wanted any part of your feud with them or theirs with you. But my brother has to go.'

'All right. It looks as though I don't have a choice. Now, why don't I let you out of here.' She took the key out of her pocket and fingered it absently for a moment. 'And then you can go back to your friends and tell them that you've got me tied up with pink ribbons.'

'I wouldn't go so far as to call you a parcel, Miss Rutherford. And they're not my friends.'

Clara unlocked the door and stood in the doorway, watching as Rennie quietly left her house.

'You haven't got a friend, captain,' she said with a small shake of the head. 'Not after tonight.'

CHAPTER TWELVE

Rennie let himself out and down a short flight of steps leading to the corrals and stables. The buckskin did not appear to be in the corral but as he entered the stable block and walked along the row of stalls, he saw a familiar bulk.

The old horse playfully butted his shoulder as he entered the stall and he fussed with his mane and spoke to him in his own private language for a minute before spreading the saddle blanket.

'You always were a little strange around horses,' a voice spoke suddenly behind him. It was Steven.

Rennie made no reply as he hefted the saddle across the buckskin and began securing it. His brother loomed out of the shadows, unshaven and dirty. His clothes reeked of smoke and the smell of kerosene.

'She told me 'bout what happened. I went to the little guest room but you'd gone.'

'Very observant of you,' Rennie answered without turning. 'Now that you've found me, what do you want?'

'I want to talk to you if you'll stand still a minute.'

Rennie turned. He looked at the face so like his own and wondered why and how it was possible to hate someone so much and yet be willing to go to almost any lengths to protect them.

'We've got nothing to say to one another,' he said in a flat, low voice, so reminiscent of their father when he was on the brink of losing his temper. 'Go back to your friends.'

'You can't ride tonight, not in that state,' Steven said roughly. He hated to be reminded of his father, a man he had betrayed and lied to and stole from all his life.

'Did you come here to commiserate with me, Steven? That's really not your style.'

'I don't like what they did to you. Why didn't you just tell them what you saw? If they'd come here we'd have been ready for them.'

'I wouldn't do that to my worst enemy. I wouldn't even do that to you, Steven,' Rennie said, angry that Steven would even suggest such a thing. He took a step closer to his brother, puzzled by that smell on him. When he realized what it was, what his brother had been doing tonight, his head went down almost in defeat. He felt exactly the same way his father had done every time he had had to bale Steven out of some fresh scrape, each one a little worse than the last, until his father finally gave up on him, conceded that Steven was beyond redemption.

'Now you listen to me, Steven,' Jim said in a cold, deadly serious tone. 'I had some words with your boss tonight and I told her that unless you and the pack of rats you run with aren't a hundred miles from here by Saturday, you'll all hang. And you know me, Steven. I'm not Dad. I don't make idle threats.'

'Come on, Jim,' Steven protested, spreading his hands. 'Don't cut us out of this deal because of what happened years ago. And don't cut yourself out. This is big. We all stand to make our fortunes here.'

'You didn't have to turn into a thief and a murderer to make a fortune. You had everything in Boston.'

'I had nothing in Boston,' Steven growled, keeping his

82

voice low, as if someone was listening. 'Nothing but cheap handouts from the old man. I hated everything he stood for and I hated Boston.'

'So you decided to make a career out of hustling women and children and torching hard-working farmers' property? Was that your big career move, Steven?'

'Well it's better than being a pig farmer,' Steven told Jim with contempt.

'You're the one left me without a choice. I can't go home and I can't be a soldier and I won't be a two-bit hustler like you, harassing innocent people. So I'm going to be a farmer. I'm going to be a good one and Steven?' He took a menacing step towards his brother. 'Don't try to mess it up for me. I could make life very, very unpleasant for you.'

'You're bluffing,' Steven said, shrugging weakly, but he did know his brother and he knew there was a relentless, unforgiving, dangerous side to him that you really didn't want to cross, not if you could avoid it.

'Go ask Kelly where he lost his crucifix. Ask Gus and Kelly where they were the morning after the Cutter barn burned down. And ask yourself where you should be right now. That's right, Steven. I went to Donahue. I asked the federal marshal, about you and he told me you had broken prison last year, half-way through a four year sentence.'

Steven's former belligerence altered dramatically to dumb surprise and fear.

'You can rely on me to keep my mouth shut,' Rennie consoled him. 'Just so long as you leave. For once in your life, Steven, do the right thing.'

Jim finished saddling the buckskin with Steven's flushed face turned towards him, his eyes jumping with panic and hatred. Rennie pulled himself into the saddle, rode a few yards, then stopped and looked back at his brother.

'Goodbye, Steven,' he said finally. 'I hope we don't meet

again, but I can come to your trial if you want, even though you couldn't stay for mine.'

He reached Creeback a little after daybreak, shredded by the exhaustion of the last twenty-four hours. He could no longer ignore the sickening back pain nor the waves of nausea and weakness that were sweeping through him in regular and increasing spasms. He was glad and relieved to see the house below for he knew that he would have to lie down soon or fall down.

He was not prepared however for the sight of a horse tethered there, nor for a smoking chimney and the strong aroma of coffee. He stared at the horse stupidly, unable to identify it, unable to think who would be here this early and who would be coolly making coffee on his stove, in his house. When Sam Cutter came out onto the porch, looking up at the horseman on the trail, Jim heaved a huge sigh of relief.

He moved down to the yard and drew rein there, looking across at his friend. He began to dismount, with such obvious discomfort that Sam hurried to help him, catching him around the waist. Once on the ground, Rennie asserted a little dignity and gently pushed Sam away.

'I'm all right,' he said and he moved towards the house. Though his legs felt weak and unsteady under him, he made it to the porch chair and carefully sat down.

'What happened to you?' Sam demanded angrily.

'Got in a fight.'

'What with, a grizzly?' Sam asked and Rennie smiled.

'Four grizzlies. It's a bit early for a social call, isn't it? Where did you get the coffee? I'm fresh out.'

'Who was it, Jim? For God's sake tell me.'

Rennie closed his eyes, but a weaving, persistent hallucination of light floated dizzily in front of him. He wished that Sam would go home and leave him alone.

'It doesn't matter,' he said, in such a lifeless tone that Sam became even more concerned.

'It matters to me. Tell me their names.'

'How about some of that coffee?'

Sam compressed his mouth and straightened away from the chair Rennie was slumped in. Exasperated, he clumped into the house, rattled the stove and coffee pot and a minute later stomped back out with two mugs. He thrust one into Rennie's hand.

'Was it Rutherford's men?' he jabbed. Rennie turned his head to appraise Sam, sitting in the corner chair now, his back to the yard, both big hands clasped around his coffee cup.

'Rutherford's men what, Sam?'

'Did that, beat the tar out of you,' Sam said without patience. Rennie said nothing. He stretched out his legs, crossing them at the ankles. If Sam persisted with his questions, he would be sadly, badly disillusioned.

'Come on, tell me. If you don't, I'm gonna fetch Cass out here and you can tell him.'

Still Rennie said nothing and Sam watched him thoughtfully, unable to understand his attitude, his stubbornness, blindly trampling over ground best left undisturbed. He could see that something profound had happened to his friend in the few short hours since he had spoken to him but he couldn't begin to guess what.

'What brought you out here at this hour of the morning, Sam?'

'Eve was worried about you. She had a bad feeling, woman's kind of thing. Frances told me I wasn't getting breakfast till I came. But you weren't here.'

Rennie pulled in a big breath and let it out slow, disturbed by the idea of Eve lying awake worrying about him.

'I was at the Rutherfords', finding out, one way and another, about why your people have been having so much trouble. Seems the railroad might be coming through here soon, cutting right across settlers' land. That south-east stretch of property of yours and about a dozen others will be worth a lot of money soon. The boy Corey found out about it and they killed him.' He took the unburned telegram from his shirt pocket and gave it to Sam. He had burned a receipt for grain in Clara's study. Sam's eyes widened when he read it but mostly he was confused.

'Tom Rutherford is a bed-ridden invalid,' Jim went on. 'His daughter deliberately crippled him because he didn't want to bring any trouble to the settlers. He's not the one who's done all those things Sam. Just Clara and my brother and a lot of hired trouble.'

'You've been a busy man,' Sam said thoughtfully.

'I told Clara I had proof against her and that it had to stop, the burning and all of it. And I spoke to my brother, just like we talked about last night.'

'And . . . he agreed to go?'

'Not in so many words. But I laid it on the line for him.'

'Was that before or after you fought with him?'

'I didn't say I fought with him, Sam, and I wish you'd just leave it alone.'

'If it wasn't Rutherford's men then who. . . ?'

Rennie came to his feet and leaned heavily against the porch rail. Anger came to him now, tight and hard in his chest.

'I'm sorry, Jim, but I'm going to find out sometime. You have to tell me.'

Jim turned and faced Sam and tried to convey with his eyes what the telling would mean. But Sam ignored the signals. He was prepared, or so he thought, and nothing could be that terrible.

'Wasn't Rutherford men, Sam,' Jim said quietly. 'It was settlers. Four of them. They were waiting for me last night in the barn.'

Sam rocked, caught completely off guard. He would have accepted anything but that, anything but his own people. They were the ones who shouted with angry voices against the tyranny of Rutherford, cried out for shame against the cruelty and violence they had wreaked on all the settlers. Now they had crawled down into the ditch alongside their enemy. They had come here to find out who had killed Corey, Sam now realized, and he shuddered to think of the consequences for all of them if Rennie had told them anything of what he knew. They would have ridden out into a massacre.

At first Sam was unable to lift his eyes. He could only shake his head, over and over.

'Your friends tied me over my horse and left me on Rutherford property. That's how I came to talk with Clara.'

'No friends of mine and God forgive for ever thinking they were. I'll never let them near my home or my family again.'

There was a brief flicker of sympathy in Rennie's eyes.

'You don't know who they were.'

'I'll find out,' Sam promised, the white heat of his anger dying down a little. After all, he wasn't the one who'd been hurt in all this. 'After I get you a doctor.'

'I don't need a doctor. I need sleep, a hot tub maybe. Garson would only ask a lot of questions that I don't want to answer right now.'

'I don't agree. You look like hell.'

'Would you just water the stock for me. Then go home.'

'Why, you stubborn, pig-headed . . . you never change,' Sam berated him, recalling suddenly an incident during the war when his captain had been wounded and had refused medical aid. They'd had a fierce tussle that day, arguing back and forth, Sam cursing him for a stubborn fool, Rennie trying to pull rank, ordering Sam to fetch his horse, his New England accent intensifying as his fever mounted. Then he had passed out, blood flooding suddenly into his chalk white face as he keeled over in a dead faint.

Sam watched as Rennie moved away from the porch rail and was not surprised when history repeated itself. Sam caught him as he went down and carried him into the house, to the bedroom in the back. He laid him down carefully, remembering how he had laid him down before on the army cot, covering him with a rough, dirty camp blanket. He wondered when he would be able to look Jim Rennie in the eye again without thinking about what his 'friends' had done to him. He drew the plain, but this time clean blanket up over him and swept his hair back off his brow with a fatherly hand.

'You sleep, Captain,' he said roughly, the same words he had used then. 'Plenty time for battles later.'

CHAPTER THIRTEEN

A little after midday, Eve spotted a solitary rider coming over the hill from the bridge and her instincts told her at once who it was. She put down her basket of washing, nearly spilling the shirts and sheets and ran to the new barn where her father worked alone.

'It's Jim,' she called to him and did not wait for his alarmed exclamation, but ran to the edge of the yard to meet him. Her father had told her what had been done to him and she experienced a heart-squeezing moment of fear that he might hate her as he was bound to hate those men.

He rode straight up to her and because the sun was behind him, his face was dark till he eased himself, with great caution, out of the saddle and down onto dry land. She saw how he gripped the pommel for support before steadying himself and turning slowly towards her. He took off his hat and she saw the ugly bruising and the scratches of his violent encounter with her father's friends.

'I'm sorry they did that to you,' she said. He looked at her with a quiet hunger, trying to remember every detail of her face and hair and colouring, the sweet pattern of freckles on her cheek and the way the light touched and was absorbed by her eyes.

'You should see the other guy,' he said with a smile,

recalling that strategically placed kick between Tom Colton's legs, in particular.

'I don't want to see them,' she said gruffly, snatching at his hat. 'Put that on. Don't you know how hot that sun is?'

'Where are they all, the men I saw the other day working on the barn?' he asked as he replaced the hot, black felt, experiencing instantly the relief it gave from the crushing heat.

'Dad told them all to go to Hell,' she said candidly.

'What about your party on Saturday? Is that all off?'

'I suppose we'll have it just the same. But today, my dad's too sore. You'd think he was the one they'd. . . .' She gave a little shrug. She wanted to put her arms around him and kiss his battered face and tell him how much she loved him but her father was walking towards them, swinging a hammer in his fist.

'I told you to stay in bed.'

'I know you did. But I'd an idea you'd send all your help away, so I came to lend a hand,' he said and he looked towards the new barn.

'I can just see you on a ladder. Look, you can hardly stand without holding on to that horse of yours.'

'I can hit a nail on the head. Don't be so stubborn. Anyway, if I stay maybe the lady of the house will take pity on me and lay an extra place at the table.' He looked at Eve. He smiled again and she smiled back, their intimacy radiating a gentle heat that even Sam could feel.

They worked all day. The sky vibrated brassily down on two sweat-saturated backs, on bared, muscular, sun-browned arms, on the saw-dust smelling wood and the soft baked yellow-brown dirt of the yard.

Rennie determinedly ignored his body's protests and blinked the burning saltiness from his eyelids, flicking his head sharply to one side so that the sweat flew. He thought that work was the answer to the effects of that body blow, but every so often the sucking blackness would reach up for his throat and he would make a grab for something till it passed.

Only this one time it failed to pass, just like this morning on the porch. Sam was watching him. With slitted eyes he saw Rennie straighten up from a spar of timber and lift one hand to his forehead, brushing back his hat to ease the tightness of the sweat band, to block out the slashing brightness of sky and sun and at that he fell. Sam swore, threw down his saw and called to the house.

'Honey, bring some water,' and he knelt and took the racing pulse. It was only a faint, just like this morning, a momentary passing out. He'd be all right in a minute. But a minute later, as the family all clustered round, Jim's eyes were still closed and Eve was quietly starting a small, private panic.

'Sam, he has to be taken in out of the sun,' a concerned Frances advised and Sam gave a grim nod and lifted him. 'Put him in Eve's room,' she called after him and she stooped to lift Rennie's fallen hat.

In the cool, dark room at the back of the house, Sam laid Jim down, draping his unmoving form with the bed cover. Rennie moved his head restlessly on the pillow and sighed, moistening his lips, wetting the chalky dryness and opened his eyes.

'So much for that idea,' he said hoarsely.

'Big talker,' Sam reproached him, but with relief in his voice.

'I'll be all right . . . in a minute.'

'Sure you will, especially since you're staying right there till I say different.'

To Sam's surprise Rennie had no arguments. He was so tired. He had not slept properly in days. He looked dreamily at Eve, who stood stiffly at the foot of the bed. A second later he was asleep.

He knew it was late when he woke because the window that looked out onto Frances Cutter's kitchen garden was dark. He sat up stiffly but was relieved to find that the tight, sawing pain in his back was almost gone. He wondered just how long he had lain there like a dead man and in the gloom he tried to read the face of the little porcelain clock beside the bed. It was seven-thirty.

The family was just sitting down to supper when he appeared in the doorway, looking much better than he had done this afternoon. He had tucked his shirt-tail in and had bathed his face and neck in the wash basin and had brushed his tousled hair with Eve's faintly scented hairbrush. Frances got up from her place and went towards him. She felt his brow with the back of her hand, her eyes filled with a genuine and, to Rennie, very touching concern.

'How do you feel?' she asked him.

'Better.'

'Well, come on and sit down to supper. I was planning on keeping you a bite, but now you're here. Are you hungry?'

'Oh, leave him alone, Mother,' Eve laughed.

'Let him catch his breath, Fran.' Sam pulled a chair out for him and rested a hand on his shoulder for a moment as he sat.

'I'm sorry it isn't a good Boston boiled dinner.' Frances cheerfully ignored them all as she took care of her guest. She served him with a plate of beef stew and potatoes and it tasted as good as anything he had ever eaten in Boston, drank almost a pitcher of milk with it and left just enough room for Eve's contribution to the meal, a Dutch apple cake, served with thick yellow cream. He ate and allowed their uncomplicated warmth and friendship to enclose him, glad and grateful to have such friends. Afterwards, Frances served tea in her prized china teaset and again Rennie felt himself drifting back on his memories.

His parents never drank coffee, only tea, from a Limoges service that cost a fortune, attended by a girl called Meg, who had been in service to his family since she was eleven years old. He remembered breakfasts of English muffins and bacon and eggs, freshly ironed newspapers and his father's strictly observed rule, that no one should speak at breakfast, except to say 'Pass the marmalade'. He recalled formal dinners, guests arriving in carriages and finery, his father's favourite dry, nutty wine being served in Waterford crystal, meals of six or seven courses, crisp, starched table linen and heavy, beautiful silver to eat with.

But when they had all gone home, there were the inevitable fights between his father and brother, about Steven's drinking and gambling, about the unsuitability of the women he went with and about money, always money, Steven's propensity for spending it and his father's increasing reluctance to give him any.

The end came with that last, terrible quarrel when Steven threatened and struck his father, wrecked the study, starting a small fire in the process, and emptied the safe. Jim stopped him, sobered him up and got the truth out of him. He owed some people a lot of money and they were out of patience with him. They wanted his money or his hide.

Jim Rennie let his brother go that night, let him take what was in the safe but told him never to come back. And he never did. Jim never saw his brother again until the day he turned up at Fort Macaulay with Gus and Kelly.

It was painful to remember. He missed his home, missed his parents and other members of his family, missed living by the coast. He had not given up that life from choice. He blinked and returned reluctantly to the present, the Cutter kitchen, the ebb and flow of their conversation around him. Sam was watching him. He knew Jim Rennie's past, knew his family were wealthy, well-connected Bostonians and knew that sometimes his friend got a faraway look in his eye, the sad look of a homesick man. He had that look tonight.

'It's probably raining in Boston right now,' he said. Rennie looked up at him and gave a soft laugh. He sometimes thought Sam knew him better than he knew himself. He glanced at the half-case clock on the kitchen wall, swallowed the last of his tea and pushed the delicate little cup away from him.

'During the war, my father wrote to me every day. He told me that every evening, at eight o'clock, just before dinner, my mother would go to a little picture she used to have of me and she would kiss it and say a little prayer. "Please let there be a meal for my son tonight, please let him have somewhere warm and dry to rest his head." I got into the way of always watching for eight o'clock and taking a minute to think about them both. I still do it.'

The others had fallen silent listening to him, and a stillness came over the little party at the table as they waited for the chime of the old clock which came just a second later, soft as a heartbeat in the silence of the room. And Jim Rennie knew, as surely as if he was standing in the drawing-room beside her, that his mother, in her finest silk gown, hair beautifully dressed and pinned, the scent of damask roses on her wrists, would be gently kissing an old faded daguerreotype of himself in a Union army uniform.

When he looked up, Eve was watching him with gentle, knowing eyes. Her scarce and treasured store of knowledge of Jim Rennie had been increased tonight a hundred fold.

'I used to do the same thing with Sam,' Frances said and her husband, unable to get his finger through the dainty handle of the tea cup and holding it like the old coffee mug he drank out of when he was working outside, gave her a speculative look. 'I used to say, "Please Lord, let Sam remember to change his socks this week".' Everybody laughed, except Sam, who looked hurt.

'I used to say that prayer too,' Rennie laughed. 'But it was never answered.'

The laughter died away and Frances started to gather the crockery together.

'But I understand, Jim,' she said, looking at her guest, 'why your mother did that. Being left at home when your loved ones are in danger isn't easy. We women have to find a way to get through it.'

They were words that would come back to haunt everyone at the table that night.

But after this pleasant evening in the company of friends, danger seemed a distant memory to Jim Rennie.

'I better get home,' he said now to Sam.

'Stay the night,' Sam suggested and their eyes met. Rennie knew why he suggested it but he shook his head.

'I can't hide behind your coat-tails forever, Sam.'

Cutter sniffed loudly and scratched his cheek, trying to think of a valid reason for keeping Jim here for at least one more night, but Rennie was already on his feet, looking around for his hat, which Andrew obligingly brought him.

'Thank you for everything, Frances. I haven't eaten so well in. . . .' He tried to remember and looked momentarily blank. 'I don't know when.'

'There's always a place for you here, Jim.'

Andrew offered to saddle the buckskin and Eve offered to walk him to the yard. With a smile at each other, Frances and Sam held back.

It was cooler outside than it had been for weeks. A breeze had sprung up from the east and it brought a breath of blessed freshness to Sam's yard. They stood at the corner of the corral and in the concealing darkness, held each other and kissed. Eve tasted the familiar, slightly sweet personal flavour of him and knew that later, when she wanted to, she would not be able to recall it exactly. Rennie felt again the dull pounding of blood to the head at the touch of her soft mouth. The sensation that he could not get his breath was not unlike his earlier experience today of fainting. Such a small thing she was to have such power over him. She kissed him back hard and in a reversal of their positions the other night, pushed him back against the corral posts.

'Don't go tonight. I-I'm scared about something,' she said, when they parted slightly. He said nothing but did not laugh at her fears.

'I have to go,' he sighed.

'Hold me tight then,' she said and he did. 'Tighter.'

'Honey, I don't want to crush you.'

'Crush me up and take me home in your pocket.'

He laughed his gentle, attractive laugh and then kissed her, his lips exploring tenderly and lovingly.

'See you tomorrow,' he promised lightly and he let her go and walked to where Andrew was holding the buckskin, pretending not to look.

'Goodnight,' he called back to the house. 'Night, Andy,' he said, riffling the boy's hair. He simply looked back at Eve, nodded to her then turned and walked up the bridge trail as far as the belt of cotton woods. He stood there for a moment to look back down at the lighted house. He could not see Eve, but he knew she was there.

He turned to mount the buckskin, hearing too late the horse's whinny of fright. The butt of the pistol took him on the corner of the chin. He heard his own sucked-in gasp of pain as he twisted into an awkward fall and then he heard nothing else except the quiet hum of senses all but switched off.

CHAPTER FOURTEEN

Sunlight slanted down from a thundery looking sky and lay in a steamy haze over the dilapidated yard. In the distance, black storm clouds were beginning to mass, piling up on one another slowly. It would take a few hours but the storm was coming.

This was one of the first sections of land Clara Rutherford had procured and the remnants of her handiwork stood forlornly before Rennie, a burnt-out barn and house and a shack that had been thrown up temporarily to house the owners just before they sold out. Rennie had been tied to what was left of the corral, his arms stretched to the limit, his wrists lashed with rawhide, strung out like washing on a line.

He had surfaced from unconsciousness hanging there and the full weight of his suspended body had bitten deep welts into his wrists. But now he was on his feet and the hide no longer bit so brutally into the lacerated flesh.

Out of half-closed eyes he watched Kelly come out of the shack and stand with a canteen in his hand, watched while he took a generous pull of water and then came strolling over. He put his fist under Rennie's chin and pushed his head back, examining the fresh bruise there where the pistol butt had connected.

'You're beginning to look like that old horse of yours,

Rennie,' he laughed. Rennie twisted his head away and the movement caused pain to rail smartly along his wrists. 'Saw you with your girl. She's sweet, a little young, but ripe I'd say.' Rennie refused to rise to the bait and Kelly changed tack. 'We brung you here to ask you a few questions, like where is my property, that little item you found after we killed the kid.'

Rennie swore bitterly and Kelly laughed and tugged at one of the thongs securing Rennie's wrists. White fire lanced along his arm, leaving him white-faced and straining.

'Move on for God's sake and give me some air.'

Kelly shrugged and viciously tested the other thong, watching with a mixture of curiosity and pleasure as spots of dark sweat appeared on Rennie's face.

'Don't expect any help, Captain. The sheriff had to leave town unexpected, and we wrote a note to your friend Sam Cutter telling him you'd gone to Donahue again for a couple of days.'

He offered no further elaboration on the subject and turned away. The big, broad, swaying shoulders reminded Rennie of Cass, riding off on a wild goose chase. What did they want him out of the way for? What lay in store for the settlers tomorrow or the next day?

With a jolt, Rennie realized that the day after tomorrow was Saturday, when all the little rabbits would be together in the one pen, at Sam's place, ready for the slaughter.

Steven and Gus arrived later. They ignored the prisoner in the yard and went directly to the shack. They had brought food with them and Tom Rutherford's brandy in a metal flask. They ate and drank, sitting at the little rickety table in the shack and then they played cards.

Steven got up after a while and stood at the door of the shack, drinking coffee, watching his brother. Kelly had suggested that they let him hang out there for the rest of the day and night and if he still wouldn't talk, they would work on

98

him a little. Gus agreed and after the merest hesitation, Steven did too.

There was nothing to do all day but sit and play cards with a greasy, marked deck, drink coffee and take turns watching Rennie grow wearier and wearier as the sun sucked the sweat off him almost before it had time to appear. They gave him a little water, but no food. It was a long day.

Gus had just announced that it was four o'clock when Clara Rutherford rode onto the property. She looked around with her habitual bored, haughty look and when Gus came to take the reins of her horse, she dismounted and walked towards her prisoner.

'Hello,' she said pleasantly to Rennie, her eyes noting with approval his swollen jaw and the bloody wrists. 'Hello again, Mr Rennie.'

Rennie opened his eyes and squinted at Clara and seeing her did nothing to raise his spirits. Her expression was one of gloating triumph.

'I had a long, hard think about what you said the other night, Mr Rennie. I wanted to help out, I really did. But in the end I decided you were simply no threat at all.'

Rennie looked over his shoulder at the three faces, all enjoying watching the woman, except for Steven, who looked morose.

'If you tell us where all the evidence is that you have, all the things that might damage us, you can go home.'

'I don't think I want to do that, Miss Rutherford. I don't want to end up at the bottom of the creek. But maybe you can tell me something. What are you going to do to the settlers?'

'Not concern for those pig farmers, surely?' she said, with a little mock shake of the head.

'Just tell me where and when and I'll make a point of not being there when it happens.'

She laughed softly and ran the edge of her thumb along

the swelling on his jaw.

'Not to worry. We'll see to that.'

Kelly, Gus and Clara rode away from the place a little after six, leaving Steven alone in the broken down shack. He topped up the last of the coffee with half the contents of the brandy flask, and when the coffee was finished, drank nearly all of the rest of the liquor, watching through the open door while Rennie sweated out the last of the day.

Evening started to draw the light and heat out of the sky and brought with it a faint, cool breeze that dried the twin mushrooms of sweat under Rennie's armpits. He looked up at the sky and his neck was stiff where the sun had beaten on it. The black cloud mass was overhead now and suddenly, within a few minutes, the cool breeze shifted into something colder, coming out of the east. Rain began to spot the yard. In a little while the sky had lost all trace of blue and was a black morass of storm, moving at speed and releasing in its wake a vertical downpour.

Rennie ducked his head and waited in miserable silence for it to pass. In the middle of this torrent he began to notice something. The water was slackening the hide fastening his left wrist, stretching it slightly. It had been inexpertly tied by Gus and now it was loosening, just a little, enough for Rennie to pull and twist it, as much as the lacerated flesh would allow until it was at the point where he could almost slip his hand free.

Steven picked that moment to come out of the shack. He was walking steadily enough and when he faced his brother and spoke to him, his voice was unaffected by the alcohol, but even in the driving rain Rennie could see the wavering candles of stupor in Steven's eyes.

'Tomorrow,' he said, raising his voice above the hiss of the storm, 'tomorrow, Kelly will hurt you. He'll hurt you in a way you wouldn't think was possible. I've seen him. And she'll be there to watch. You've got to speak up now, for God's sake, Jim.'

'What do you care what happens to me, Steven? Huh? You didn't care a damn at Fort Macauley.'

'Don't bring up Fort Macauley,' Steven warned him.

'You took everything from me that night, my career, my future and my reputation, and now you expect me to just forget it?'

'You mean the same way you took everything away from me that last night in Boston, when you threw me out, told me never to come back? Believe me brother, we're even.'

'You deliberately wrecked my life because I—'

'Because you wrecked mine. I only needed a little money to pay Jack Vincent off, but you turned me out without it.'

'You had the contents of the safe as I recall.'

'I was six hundred dollars short. This is what Vincent did to me that night.' He pulled his shirt out of his pants and revealed a scar that was eight or ten inches long, running from navel to hip. It was white and dimpled, had gone untreated at the time and still caused Steven massive pain at times, especially when he had been in the saddle for any length of time. It was a constant reminder to him of what he had done and what he had lost that night in Boston, but typically of him he did not blame the man who had almost eviscerated him. He blamed only one person for his troubles and that person was here in front of him now. Rennie's eyes tightened with pain at the sight of it but then he shook his head. He felt no guilt for what had become of his brother.

'I didn't make you gamble away everything you had. I didn't force you to turn into a thieving, no account—'

Steven hit him a backhanded punch and before another came, Rennie twisted his hand free, balled his fist and hit Steven just below the heart, with all the weight he could muster. Steven fell sideways into the mud and Rennie turned to the other thong and with cold, wet fingers and teeth, freed his other hand.

There would be a weapon in the shack. He began to head in that direction but his legs felt so feeble that he sank to his knees, got up and lurched another step or two then went down again. The second time he got up he walked straight in to Steven's fist. Before he hit the ground, his brother was on top of him.

Nobody would have paid money to see that fight. Rennie was exhausted and Steven was drunk, so drunk that even a man who had been strung out in the sun all day could and did outstrip him.

They pummelled one another for ten gruelling minutes, a vertical sheet of rain drowning their grunts and gasps as random blows connected. A final lucky punch put an end to it. Rennie put all his remaining strength into a ferocious haymaker that, unlike his last three or four blows, finally hit the target. He felt his knuckles connect with bone and Steven went down on his face in the mud. The rain drummed on his back. He did not rise.

Rennie filled his lungs three and four times and then drove himself onto his feet. His legs and arms were leaden weights and deadened with cold. He staggered to the shack and collapsed into a chair, waiting for a minute till the horrible fatigue eased a little. He drank some of Steven's brandy and then went out again, dragged his brother by the belt of his pants up out of the rain into the doorway of the shack. He took the .45 he found on the table then walked around the place in an ever-widening circle in search of transport. But there was no horse. They had evidently intended that Steven would not desert his post, no matter what. Jim had no earthly idea where he was, except that he was somewhere north of Creeback.

The rain drove into his face as he walked in what he hoped was a southerly direction, his wrists bleeding, numb with hunger and fatigue and the dull pain of too many blows. But something drove him on, a core of inner bloody-mindedness that a few people down the years, especially in the army, had seen in Rennie, despite his placid exterior. That night it probably saved his life.

The first place he hit was Tom Colton's spread. It was going on three in the morning and Rennie had reached the end of his rope. Had the entire Apache nation been hot on his heels, he couldn't have gone another step. He stumbled over a picket fence and staggered up to the house and porch and was summoning up the energy to knock when his laboured breathing was interrupted suddenly by a wracking, exhausted cough.

The house door opened without any warning. Colton had neglected to light a lamp but he had remembered his revolver and seeing a bedraggled, crouching man on his porch, thumbed the hammer and fired a warning shot into the yard.

'I'll give it you straight. Turn around and get off my property or I'll shoot you in the stomach, knees or anywhere else I can cripple you.'

As it stands, Rennie thought, I probably wouldn't feel a thing.

'Shoot me now and you'll never know who killed Corey,' he said and Colton, recognizing his voice, moved closer.

'Oh, it's you,' he said venomously. 'They've really got you on the payroll, haven't they.'

Colton took hold of his arm and turned him around, shoving him down the steps. He tripped and sprawled, up to his neck in dirt again and because he wanted to avoid a boot in the ribs, he rolled and pushed himself onto his feet. Colton was a step behind him and he jabbed Rennie's back with the revolver, all the way to the barn.

'What is it, Tom?' a frightened female voice called out.

'Nothing,' Colton shouted back forcefully. 'I'm taking care

103

of some vermin. Get the coffee on.'

The house door shut with a slam. Colton punted Rennie into the barn with a final, powerful push, and while he was again picking himself up, Colton lit a lamp and hung it from a chain attached to an overhead beam. The soft, swaying light dragged shadow and alternate light across their faces, Colton's tense and angry, Rennie's dirty and bloody and swollen. He fell against a wall, unable to stand unsupported.

'I didn't come here to hurt anybody,' he said, pressing a hand to his side.

'Are you sick, Rennie?'

'They were holding me prisoner, some deserted settlement north . . . north of here.'

He saw Colton shake his head in wonder.

'You're a damned liar, Rennie. I bin saying that about you all along. Now what the hell did they send you here for?'

'Questions,' Rennie said tiredly. 'Always questions.' He had finally realized the hopelessness of talking to this man. 'Get Sam Cutter. I'll tell him,' he said and Colton, shaking his head again, pulled a length of rope from a loose sack of grain and advanced on Rennie, intending to bind him.

Rennie held out his arms unresistingly and it was then that Colton saw the livid bites in the flesh caused by the rawhide. And stuck in the front of Jim's belt was a Colt .45. Like a man seeing the chasm he was inches from falling into, Colton paused, blinked and then lifted the weapon to check if it was loaded, which it was. He had been too hot-headed mad to search for one at the start. Rennie could have pulled it any time. With a wondering sigh he tucked the gun into his own pants.

'What is this game of yours, Rennie? I wish I knew.'

Rennie, seeing he was not to be tied after all, let his arms fall to his sides.

'I only wish it was a game, Tom.'

CHAPTER FIFTEEN

Tom Colton's boy Brad found the Cutter home in the stormy darkness with little difficulty for he was a regular visitor here, circumstances permitting. Andrew Cutter was his best friend and Brad looked upon Sam as kind of an uncle.

His small fists beat out a tattoo on the door of the house, but it was all but drowned out by the rush and howl of the storm. Something out in back of the place rattled and Brad shivered inside his heavy winter coat, which his mother had tussled with him to put on, and pounded again on the door. This time a light crept past one of the windows and a voice hollered to him, demanding his name and his business.

'It's me, Brad. Brad Colton,' he amended, realizing they couldn't see him or even hear him that well behind the stout, well-made door. 'My pa sent me.'

The sound of a bolt being drawn was lost in the drumming of a fresh squall of rain on the roof of the house. When the door was eventually yanked open, Brad blinked, slightly surprised, before Sam pulled him indoors.

A trio of anxious faces met him, Sam and Frances and Eve. In a minute Andrew appeared in his bedroom doorway, yawning, astonished to see Brad.

'Something wrong at your place, son?'

'Yesir. My pa'd be obliged if you could come.' Feeling just

a shade important to be bringing this news, Brad ignored Andrew and spoke directly to the man of the house. 'We had a prowler. Paw caught him and took him in the barn.'

With a shake of the head, Sam drew on his pants and pulled on the shirt he had worn earlier that Frances had been mending.

'Who was this prowler, Brad? Somebody from Rutherfords?'

'No sir,' Brad said emphatically. 'It was that man from Creeback, you know, Jim Rennie. His wrists were all cut up and he was carryin' a gun but he didn't try to use it on Pa. Pa can't figure it, wants to see you right away.'

The news might as well have been conveyed with a dousing of cold water. Sam sat down to pull on his boots and to hide the anger in his face. He knew that damned letter was wrong, but had ignored his own instincts. He shoved his arms into the coat Frances was holding for him.

'Didn't he go to Donahue then?' she asked him quietly and Sam curtly shook his head.

'They must have got him,' he said and they both looked at a white-faced Eve.

'Dad, I'm com—'

'No, you're not,' he told her sharply. 'If he's hurt I'll bring him back with me. Don't worry. Lock the door behind me and go to bed. I don't know how long I'll be.'

When he reached Colton's place, he found the head of every other homestead there, assembled in the parlour and kitchen, crowding the low-ceilinged rooms with their bulk. Colton was busily telling them how Rennie had arrived, looking as if he had been strung out in the storm, which he had.

'Now he's sayin' he can tell us how to stop Rutherford.'

At this the settlers fell silent. Hope, never far below the troubled surface of their lives, came shining into their eyes.

'I don't trust him for myself,' Colton said, 'but I figured you'd all want to know what he has to say.'

A ripple of speculation ran around the group, some of them nodding eagerly, some of them shaking their heads, thinking like Colton that Rennie was not to be trusted.

Having said his piece, Colton brought Rennie in from the bedroom. He was drugged with pain and stiffened by his wet clothes and the fight with Steven and that long walk through the night. He leaned against the doorjamb and dragged his eyes into focus. There were about two dozen men crowded into those small rooms and as if they were one they all turned and stared at Rennie. There was a moody, expectant silence in the room, an atmosphere as tight as a drum and it communicated itself to him at once. He found himself slowly straightening up, pushing his shoulders back and lifting his chin. There was something about the air in this room that smelt just like the air in that long ago courtroom and the eyes fixed on him bore the same look of waiting, of expectancy. His superior officers had hoped that Rennie would be cleared that day, that the facts that seemed so obvious to those who knew him would also be obvious to the men making the judgements. It hadn't turned out that way. Now a herd of grizzled farmers, dressed in homespun and workboots, smelling the earthy smell of men who worked with the soil, waited with that same look, that same hope. Only they had more to lose than the loss of a brother officer.

He noticed Sam at the back, watching him with a worried face. Sam moved slowly through the press of bodies to stand in front of his friend.

'Jim, I thought that letter was genuine. I'm sorry.'

'I was visiting with Clara Rutherford for a while. She gave me the same welcome I got one night from four of you.'

An awkward silence encased the men in Colton's parlour, guaranteeing their complicity in what had been done that night to him, in his own home. And inexplicably he thought of the valley then, as it had been that night, soft and blurry in the twilight, or as it would be now, wrapped in the rain, water pooling in that hole in the yard he had been forever meaning to fill in. He just wanted to be left alone to get on with his life and he realized that most of these men wanted the same. Some of them even deserved it.

So he told them all that had happened in the last few days, told them why Corey died, why Clara wanted their land. He told them how he had found Rutherford a cripple, a prisoner in his own home, his ranch turned into an armed camp to feed the greed and cruelty of his daughter and her friends. He told them what was going to happen to them on Saturday and he told them what they could do about it.

They listened, grave and silent and when he was finished, they began talking to one another in excited voices. It had been a long time since someone offered them a way out of their troubles.

Rennie left them to mull it over and returned to the bedroom. He stretched out on the blissfully comfortable big bed, too damned tired to care whether they believed him or not. He opened his eyes a second later, or so it seemed and there was a funny silence in the house. Then he realized that the rain and wind had died away and all he could hear was something rapidly dripping outside.

He returned to the parlour and found the settlers all gone. In the kitchen, sitting at the table drinking coffee were Sam and Tom Colton. Rennie sat down at the table with them.

'So they called your bluff,' Sam said sternly.

'They did indeed.'

'This plan of yours sounds fine. But I have one question.'

Rennie knew what the question was. Slowly and methodically he began to unwind the light bandaging that had been applied to his wrists by the Colton women.

108

'Where are you going to be when all this is happening?'

Rennie looked up. He saw that Sam already knew the answer.

'I'm going back,' he said.

'You can't,' Sam shook his head. 'There isn't any way I'm going to let you go back there.'

'You know I have to Sam.'

'I don't know any such thing. You're as good as dead if you do.'

Rennie leaned back in his chair, rubbing a hand over his tired face, really too weary for any argument.

'Cutter's right, you know,' Tom Colton said reluctantly. 'Why don't you just disappear for the next couple of days?'

'If I don't go back,' Rennie explained patiently, 'they'll know I've told you about Saturday. They'll just change their plans. If I don't go back, they'll kill Tom Rutherford, and I promised him I'd get him out of there.'

The other two men sat in uncomfortable silence, knowing that he was right and hating him to be so right.

'It'll be all right,' he said directly to Sam. 'You'll take care of everything on Saturday?'

'You know I will,' Sam said grimly and Colton half expected him to add the word 'sir'.

'Well, that seems to be settled then,' Jim said, smiling unconvincingly. 'I'll leave in an hour or so. I don't suppose there's any chance of a bite to eat before I go, Tom?'

'Sure, you've earned it,' Colton said grudgingly, surprised to be called by his first name.

'That's right, Tom,' Sam said with bitter irony. 'The condemned man always gets to eat a hearty meal.'

Colton got up from the table and went to speak to his wife, who was in the children's room.

'What in hell's name is the matter with you,' Sam demanded urgently as soon as the other man had left the

109

room. 'One minute you couldn't give horseshit for the settlers, the next you're throwing yourself out of high windows to save them.'

'This isn't about settlers, Sam.' Rennie said in a low voice. 'This is about Fort Macauley. This is about my brother. I'm putting a stop to it now and I need to know that you're with me. Are you with me, Sam?'

'You know I am.' It took Sam a while to reply but when he did he said it like he meant it.

Colton came back into the room and his petite, blonde-haired wife, Ada, came with him to fix a meal for Jim Rennie. She rustled up a plate of food that a prince would have been pleased to sit down to, said it was just leftovers and poured him a beer to go with it. Then she sat down with a cup of tea for herself and began asking Sam about Frances and the children, just as if it was a regular, everyday visit.

Rennie ate slow and drank half of the beer. He thanked Mrs Colton for her kindness, nodded to her husband, who nodded back, not hostile any more but just not friendly, and Jim and Sam left the warm, safe little kitchen. On a borrowed horse, Jim Rennie rode with Sam back the way he had come, the two of them silent, Sam still trying to think of some other way for his friend, Rennie too tired to think at all. He did wonder briefly what they might do with him when they found him, but eventually he lapsed into a little half-sleep, his head nodding. At least whatever happened he was bound to get some rest.

CHAPTER SIXTEEN

It had been arranged that everyone would meet at sunup at the burned out settlement. Kelly and Gus arrived together first, leading an extra pony for Steven. Neither man had been to bed. They had spent the night playing cards and whoring and drinking mescal at the most disreputable place in town, a place so thoroughly bad that Sheriff Cass had already decided it had to be shut down. He didn't want his town becoming that kind of town.

And from quite a distance away the gunmen could see that Rennie was no longer strung up between the corral posts. They reined in to look at one another and then continued on up to the little shack, each hopeful that maybe Steven had taken pity on his brother and had brought him in out of the rain. But Steven was lying where Jim Rennie had left him, in an alcoholic stupor, his clothes still damp from the storm and blood around a cut on his eyebrow hardened to a thick crust.

'Wake him up,' Kelly barked at Gus while he made a quick tour around the place, still hopeful that a partially disabled Rennie might be lying out back somewhere. He returned to find Steven sitting in the doorway, nursing his aching head and staring down at his mud-yellowed boots. Gus shoved a flask of hot coffee into his hand and he pressed it to his cheek.

'Look, I'm sorry he got away,' he said sullenly. Kelly flicked a contemptuous glance at him and sighed deeply down through his nostrils.

'You're a stupid asshole,' he said, 'but I should have had more sense'n to leave a man to guard his own brother.'

Steven lifted his head and concentrated his one good eye on Kelly.

'What's that supposed to mean?' he demanded and Kelly gave an insolent shrug.

'He just means he should've known the captain would take advantage when you were alone,' said Gus quickly, gauging accurately the beginnings of a row between them that might end in something more than harsh words.

'Let's just forget it,' Kelly said, 'and try and figure out what we're gonna tell the woman.' With this Kelly smiled and poked his tongue into his cheek at the thought of Clara with her blood up. 'She'll be here any minute now to watch the fun.'

Steven and Gus exchanged glances, not relishing the prospect of Clara arriving and finding out they'd let her prize catch off the hook.

And when she came she was not at all pleased that Rennie was gone. She cursed all three of them roundly, in language she had not learned at finishing school, and paced the yard, her head bent in concentration.

Kelly watched her, arms folded, eyes appreciatively following the movements of her shapely hips and legs. She was wearing pants today and polished riding boots and a soft white shirt open at the throat.

'He'll more'n likely make for his friend's place,' he said. She spun slowly on a high-heeled boot and appraised Kelly, one eyebrow lifted.

'Sam Cutter?'

'Yes, ma'am. They're thick as thieves. Near as I can figure,

112

Cutter was the only one believed him when he said he never saw what happened to Corey.'

'Yes. I want a lookout there. Gus can do that.'

Gus nodded. Personally he liked looking at the Cutter girl better than the starchy Miss Rutherford. He had been keeping an eye on Eve Cutter for some little time now and had promised himself that one day, when the Cutters' turn came, he would show her all the things those sweet little whores in Charleston and Savannah had shown him.

'Or he might head for his own place, but I don't think. . . .'

'You don't think he'd be that stupid?' Clara nodded, smiling. 'You're right not to underestimate him, Kelly. He's smarter than any one of you and he probably thinks he has nothing left to lose. Personally, I think he'll have gone looking for a horse to get to town or to Donahue. I don't think he'll go within a hundred miles of Sam Cutter. He's loyal that way. Steve, you can keep a lookout at Creeback Valley. You and I, Kelly, we'll scout around the immediate area. He probably didn't get that far on foot. He wasn't looking in the best physical state yesterday.' She said this last with a pointed look at Steven, her accusation that he should not have let a man in such a weak condition get the best of him plain to see.

'Yes, ma'am,' Kelly said and he inclined his head to the two men. When they had ridden away, he turned and fixed Clara with a cool stare, which she returned. She was hardly in the mood for his idea of fun and games, not now.

'You start at the south end, working west,' she told him and he shifted himself from the fence he had been leaning on, slouching lazily across her path. As he reached her side he slipped a hand across her stomach and around her waist. She turned her head and looked at him in cold surprise.

'What are you doing?'

'I'm working up to kiss you,' he stated.

113

Clara laughed harshly and Kelly kissed her open mouth with brutal strength. For a moment she found herself responding and her hand caught his shoulder and squeezed hard. He had been drinking and smoking and had three days growth on his chin but he had a magnetism, a scarcely leashed animal power that Clara had been drawn to right from the word go. She knew he was capable of great cruelty, but not with her. They were cut from the same cloth.

He drew back, his lower lip clinging to hers for a moment, then he let her go, satisfied that he had made his mark. She was breathless, her colour high. Just for a minute there she had thought he was going to take her here, out in the open, in the derelict yard of a homestead they had destroyed between them. She would have like that. He liked taking risks and she liked taking them with him.

'I think you ought to go home, Miss Rutherford, and let me take the south area,' he said, drawing on his leather work gloves. It was their little joke, that he still called her Miss Rutherford. 'He's got Steve's gun and he might be an officer and a gentleman, but he's desperate and he might be likely to forget you're a lady.'

By this time Clara had recovered her composure.

'Why, Kelly,' she said. 'Are you by any chance telling me what to do?'

'No, ma'am, not me,' he grinned at her. 'But I think he's headed south and it's probably best if I find him first.'

Kelly soon found as he rode south that the heavy rains had obliterated anything that might have been a trail. He rode slowly, smoking a cigarette, recalling with pleasure the fierce way the woman had kissed him back, her barely suppressed passion and the soft yielding of her breast as he held her close. With luck he could make life very easy for himself here. All he had to do was find the captain.

He found him thirty minutes later. To Kelly it seemed that

he must have blundered over the edge of a gully in the darkness, knocking himself senseless, for there he lay, face down in a shallow pool of dirty water.

Kelly slid unhurriedly down the slope towards him and turned him over, half expecting him to be dead, drowned or with a broken neck. He was, of course, neither one, just convincingly grimy, an effect achieved by rolling over a few times in the mud while Sam Cutter kept a safe distance to avoid being splashed. The exhaustion in his face was real enough, however, and there was no pretence when Kelly lifted what felt like a dead weight and struggled back up the slope to put Rennie over the front of his horse.

'She's gonna love me for this,' Kelly said, clapping Rennie on the back as he turned the horse towards the ranch.

In his hiding place, Sam Cutter reluctantly lowered the rifle he had trained on Kelly and with a heavy heart turned for home. He could have taken Kelly where he sat and brought Jim Rennie out of there to safety, but killing him would have made no odds. Clara had another dozen on the ranch just like him. Rennie was right. They had to end it on Saturday, once and for all.

CHAPTER SEVENTEEN

Clara had not been prepared to take any chances with Jim Rennie this time. She had him put in the cellar, a windowless, stone-floored room that had no lock but could be stoutly barred on the outside. There was wine stored here on specially built racks, kegs of beer and apples and vegetables for the winter. It ran almost the length of the entire house and except for three long narrow chinks of light that came from a grating somewhere close to the kitchens, it was uniformly dark.

After waking on the hard floor with a monstrous headache and fierce, burning pain in both wrists, Rennie gave himself a little guided tour, realized quickly that he was not getting out of here without help and settled down on a stack of burlap sacks to wait. After a while he started to feel chilled for the cellar was really just one huge cold store. He pulled some of the sacks around himself and tried sleep. Then he heard the door being unbarred and somebody was standing in the doorway, holding a shotgun.

'On your feet, soddy,' Kelly said and with a dull, slow beat of the heart, thinking he had finally outlived his usefulness in the keeping quiet stakes, Rennie stood up and followed Kelly up the stairs to the main part of the house.

It was evening. The lamps in the house were lit and even their mellow light hurt his eyes for a time. Kelly walked him to the dining-room, where Clara and Steven and Gus were seated, having just finished a sumptuous evening meal. They were enjoying snifters of brandy now, Steven smoking a thin cigar. They had been laughing about something when Kelly ushered Rennie into the room.

'Good evening, Mr Rennie. I hope you've not been too uncomfortable downstairs,' Clara said pleasantly. Rennie was tired of these little sparring sessions with her, tired of her villainy dressed up as civilized behaviour. He looked at her as if she had crawled out from under a rock and the indulgent smile on her face melted away. Then he looked at his brother. Steven returned the look, hating to see him degraded this way, dirty and unshaven and tired.

'What are you doing here, Steven? What are you doing with these people?'

'Jim, don't—'

'Our parents should see you now, sitting down to the same table as a murderer and a whore.'

Deliberately provocative, he knew somebody would react and he felt the slightest movement behind him. Kelly didn't mind being called a murderer but he didn't like to hear a lady being called a dirty name.

As he moved to punish Rennie, fist bunched, he walked straight into an elbow, travelling back with brutal force. It connected with the bone between his eyes and Kelly saw a galaxy of bright lights and then abrupt blackness. Rennie vaulted his toppling body and sprinted out of the room, hauling the door shut behind him. The door opened outwards, which he had noticed as they came in, and he jammed it shut with a chair, then went up the stairs three at a time. He burst into Rutherford's little garret, giving the man

117

in the bed an unpleasant jolt.

'Rutherford, it's Jim Rennie,' he said urgently and heard in response an expelled sigh of relief.

'So you finally came back,' he growled, trying to hide that relief.

'They've been holding me in the cellar. They brought me up a minute ago, I don't know why. I smashed Kelly's nose and broke away. They'll be here in a minute.'

'You're a subtle bastard, I'll give you that,' Rutherford conceded. He sat up a little to look at Rennie and didn't like what he saw at all. Jim had kept his word and come back but at what cost.

'I've warned the settlers that your daughter plans to wipe them out on Saturday. I told them to be ready. I'll try to get you out of here but if I don't come. . . .'

'You mean if they kill you.'

'Well, we have to consider every possibility, Mr Rutherford.'

'I wish you'd consider the possibility of calling me Tom.'

Rennie nodded and smiled briefly then turned and went to the door. He listened. It sounded as if somebody was using a battering ram on the door downstairs. He returned to the bed.

'If I don't come, Sam Cutter knows to bring the sheriff and the other settlers and the whole damn town if necessary.'

'That's good, son. But you'll come for me, won't you.'

'Don't . . . count on it. Just don't count on anything where your daughter and her friends are concerned.'

There was a crash below them and Rutherford waved an urgent hand at him.

'Go on, get out of here while you can.' Rennie nodded but had no intentions of trying to escape. He had only wanted to warn Rutherford. He unlocked the door and was about to slip out, then paused and returned to the bed.

'Where did Forrest hide the spur and broken strap?'

118

'There's a big ugly vase in my old room. He dropped them inside it.'

Rennie nodded, thinking the items were probably safest there for the time being. He nodded, clasped Rutherford's hand in farewell and let himself out of the attic room.

On the first floor corridor he moved quickly to a window he had checked out on his last visit. It led out onto a small ledge. He climbed out, closing the window behind him and made an easy climb down, stepping from the ledge to a broad window frame and then down onto a water butt and jumping from there to the ground.

Then he ran, in no particular direction, just away from the house, towards a cluster of buildings, the bunkhouse he supposed. He could hear a commotion behind him, shouts and orders. He ducked behind a building and looked back, his chest heaving, wondering how to distract the search party. Then he had an idea that brought a smile to his face.

He ran for the barn and made it inside before anyone saw him. There was feed and hay in here, but no livestock, just lots of flammable material. He found a lantern, lit it, waited until the glass was good and warm and then threw it up into the hayloft. At first there was nothing, then a little smoke and then suddenly the bright glow of fire.

He made a break for the door and this time ran towards the stable block. He crouched in the shadows, watching the barn and with a little nod of pleasure, saw a great cloud of black smoke pour out of the barn door. A moment later flames shot through the roof and suddenly they weren't looking for him any more, suddenly there was panic and yelling and boots thudding on the ground as everybody went to the fire.

'That's for Sam Cutter,' he said softly. Then he let himself into the stables, went down the line looking for the buckskin. He hoped the old horse was here but he wasn't hopeful. He whistled low and heard a snort of recognition further down the line. As he reached the buckskin, heartily glad to see the old boy, a tall thin fellow with a cigarette on his lip stepped out of the shadows. Before Rennie had time to register who it was, he took a back-handed punch that laid him out cold on the floor.

He came to with the arrival of Kelly and Gus, who man-handled him to his feet, twisting his arms fiercely up his back.

'Good work, Alder,' Kelly said to the hired man, who moved forward into the light now, to look at the intruder he had slugged. It was only then that he recognized the young man he had found tied over his horse. He looked right into Rennie's eyes and seemed to apologize with his, just a flicker of regret, but Rennie was sure he saw it, just before briefly passing out again, his head lolling forward.

Feeling the slackness of his limbs, Kelly stooped and let Rennie's body fall across his shoulders and carried him back up to the house, past the burning barn, the fire nearly under control now.

He laid Rennie down on the sofa and stood back to look at him. His own eye was beginning to blacken with that crude elbow punch, but he admired him for making a run for it. He would have done the same himself. As for nearly burning the barn down, that was a nice touch.

Clara came into the room flustered and angry, her breasts heaving. Her carefully dressed hair had started to come down around her pretty ears. Steven followed in behind her, bewildered by his brother's stupidity. Every time he tried to protect him, tried to stop the others from killing him, he went off and did something like this.

She picked up a pitcher of iced water from the dining table and threw it over Rennie and watched him come out of it, half-drowned now, his eyes blinking painfully open to the familiar faces around him.

'Get him up,' she said, her teasing, playful tone of earlier in the evening gone for good. They lifted him and had to hold him up because his legs wouldn't support him.

'Where was he?' she asked Kelly.

'Stables. Alder stopped him.'

'Alder? But he isn't—' She shook her head, letting the thought go. 'Mr Rennie, you are beginning to be more trouble than you are worth.'

'Well, Miss Rutherford,' he said, mimicking her let's-be-friends tone of earlier. 'How does it feel to watch your barn go up in flames?' Her angry response was to hit him, another back hander that worsened Alder's cut, causing blood to flow, smearing her hand and his cheek.

'I suppose you know what they do to barn-burners around these parts, Mr Rennie?' she asked him.

'Hasn't deterred you so far,' he replied, deliberately goading her and enjoying it. Kelly gave his arm a playful twist and he caught his breath, silenced for the minute. Clara swept a hand up over her hair, smoothing away some loose strands, and drew a deep, calming breath.

'There's no need to act so superior, Mr Rennie. After all, you've failed in just about everything you've attempted to do. You threatened us and you failed. You tried to escape Steve and you failed and if you'll take a look outside you'll see that you couldn't even manage to burn down my barn. You were a loser at Fort Macauley and you're a loser now.'

'That's right, Miss Rutherford. My brother is the big success story in my family.' He turned to look at Steven and saw only petulance and impatience on his face.

'Put him back in the cellar, boys,' she said, turning away to pour herself a large brandy.

As they led Rennie away he permitted himself a very small smile of relief. He had convinced her that he had failed to escape from Steven, failed to warn his friends and so long as they all went on thinking that, he could put up with the cellar and just about anything else that was coming his way.

CHAPTER EIGHTEEN

On Saturday, a day as hot as any that summer, Gus and one of Clara's hired men, Roy Sharp, watched from the thick shadows of a stand of chestnut trees as the Burrows family packed food and drink onto the back of their flat-bed wagon and, decked out in their best clothes, drove down onto the track leading to town and Sam Cutter's barn-raising. As the wagon rounded a curve and was lost to sight, Gus nodded to the other man.

'We'll give them five minutes,' he said and he drew out his tobacco pouch and rolled himself a smoke, stuck it into the corner of his mouth and lit it, screwing up one eye as the smoke trickled upwards. The hired man, who had been sitting, shifted into a crouch and checked for the third time that his rifle was loaded.

'This is too easy,' he said and Gus laughed.

'Stop worrying. Come on, let's do it.'

He left the shadows, walking casually into open sunlight and snapped the cigarette away into the dust of the yard. He approached the house with the ease of a man walking to his own porch. Sharp followed behind carrying a can of coal oil. The nervous look on his face had deepened as he found himself out in the open. This was the second time he had been on a job with Gus and he had already decided that it would be the last. He wasn't cut out for this kind of thing.

Gus turned to look at him and snatched the can of coal oil out of his sweating hands and began to throw the oil liberally over the porch and house walls. And then the house door opened with a tiny squeak and the barrel of a rifle poked out.

'Drop that can,' a voice told him. The nervous Sharp turned on his heel and started running and the rifle spoke twice, bringing the hired man down in a shock of blood from a bad shoulder wound. While the shots were being fired, Gus took his chance to duck and run in the opposite direction and was going strong for the trees when a sixteen-year-old boy, sweat running in a river down his face, came out through the door, pausing to check that the man on the ground was going to give him no further trouble before raising the rifle and finding Gus in his sights. The boy was a fair shot. That was why, despite his mother's protests and tears, he had been left behind, but even he could not have predicted this outcome, for Gus was still holding the can of coal oil and some if it had splashed him. The boy fired twice, as he had done with Sharp and the second bullet hit the oil can and ignited it.

Gus went up like a Roman candle, a human torch, still running, but from the first bullet, a dead man. When he finally fell in flames, thrashing in the dust, screaming as he was consumed, the boy ran to him and stood off to one side, watching with detached interest as the skin blackened and curled like burning paper, exposing red flesh below which also quickly blackened. The stench was terrible.

The boy felt no pity as he watched Gus in his death throes. One of his friends had died in his burning cabin, torched by one of these men and he hadn't been given any warning.

Finally, when it was over, he kicked some dust on the smoking blackened corpse, with its characteristic boxer's pose, a token gesture for his parents, who would ask if he had tried to help.

'Well, you was goin' to Hell someday, anyway,' he said to the unfortunate Gus and then with a little breath of relief he turned away, glad that it was over, that he had played his part in Jim Rennie's plan and had played it pretty damn good.

On the other homesteads the same situation was being played out and in fact Gus and Sharp were the only casualties. Clara's men had gone in expecting no form of resistance at all but the settlers, having been forewarned, had been emphatically forearmed.

At the Cutter place the farm people milled about, trying to look as if they were having a good time, but most of them were wondering if their homes were about to go up in a blazing bonfire, or if their menfolk were now dead or wounded. Some of them wondered if it had been wise to trust Jim Rennie at all.

And on the ridge above, concealed by the little group of cottonwoods, three people sat watching. Clara, in her green riding habit, her hair held back in a net, a flat brimmed black hat casting a thick bar of shadow across her eyes; at her side, smoking one of his thin, poisonous cigarettes was Kelly, his eyes flinty as he surveyed the scene below.

'Something's wrong,' he said, turning to look at Steven, who sat on his left and who had already come to the same conclusion.

'Why aren't the boys here?' Clara asked Kelly. The boys she referred to were the men she had sent to burn out the settlers homes, who should have regrouped here half an hour ago to launch the second stage of her plan, which was to cause mayhem on Sam Cutter's spread.

'I've been counting heads down yonder,' Kelly informed her. 'We're about fifteen or twenty head short, all men.'

'What are you getting at?' Clara glared at him.

'Looks like we're missing a few party guests. You know what I think? I think our friend the captain managed to get a little

124

further away the other night than we figured. I think he told them what to expect and I don't think our boys will be joining us.'

'He wouldn't come back deliberately to us knowing we might—' Clara glanced at Steven. 'Would he?'

'He might,' Steven said harshly. 'He'd enjoy being a martyr. I think Kelly's right.'

'Well, damn his eyes,' she said in a cold fury. 'He'll pay for this.'

'I'll go scout around the settlements, see what I can find out. Steve, get down to the bridge, see who crosses into town. Don't let anybody see you.'

He started to tell Clara what she was to do, but she stopped him with a curt movement of the hand.

'I'm going back to the ranch. Meet me back there when you can.'

'Yes, ma'am,' he agreed with a smile, knowing what she had in mind. 'You take care now.'

'Don't you worry about me, Kelly. Mr Rennie is the one who's in trouble.' She looked at Steven and gave the merest shrug of the shoulders. 'I'm sorry, Steve. I'm all through being patient with him because he's your brother.'

Steven didn't answer. He looked down at the settlement one more time, and then he turned and rode down the slope towards the bridge. Behind him Clara jerked the reins of her horse cruelly and rode off in the opposite direction, leaving Kelly alone on the ridge calmly and methodically building himself a fresh smoke.

In the cellar Rennie tried and failed to get some sleep. Kelly and Gus had tied his two wrists behind him this time and had fastened the rope to a metal ring set in the wall, leaving him without enough slack to lie down. And inevitably the rope started to rub and irritate his lacerated wrists till the slow pounding of blood through them felt as if it was in his head.

125

Eventually, despite the discomfort, he fell into an exhausted, troubled sleep, events of the last few days at last overtaking him as he went down into broken darkness.

There, in the smoky hinterland of the past, he relived his own small part in the battle of Antietam and felt again the shocking, fiery pain of the bullet that almost ended his military career there and then as it gouged a path through the fleshy upper part of his left arm.

The dream brought him with a jerk back to consciousness, his head up, listening and looking towards the door, though it was too dark to see. Something had woken him, a sound from over there. The door opened, admitting a wedge of light and a tall, thin figure who came down the stairs and across the cellar floor at a leisurely pace, a cigarette in his mouth drawing a red arc as he stopped under the low beams.

Rennie felt a rough hand on the back of his neck, pushing him forward, then with one clean movement the rope that bound him to the wall was sliced. He was helped to his feet. Rennie realized then that it was Alder who stood before him, coolly folding up his pocket-knife and putting it away.

'Them wrists need some lookin' to,' he said, seeing fresh blood on Rennie's cuffs as he removed the cut ends of the rope. 'Are you all right, son?'

'Thanks,' Rennie managed, rubbing his arms, which had cramped.

'M'name's Alder. Mr Rutherford sent me to look for you. I figured they'd've put you in here, either that or in a nice deep hole in the yard.'

'I think they were saving that for later,' Rennie nodded.

'Well, are you ready to bust out of this here fruit cellar? Or was you plannin' on winterin' down here?'

'I hate to appear ungrateful, Alder, but aren't you the one that put me here in the first place?'

'I'm real sorry about that, boy. Truth is I thought you were

126

your brother. I've bin waitin' for months for a chance to get him on his own, get him for what he did to a young friend of mine. I figured in all the confusion, the fire an' all, nobody'd notice if I took care of him.'

Rennie smiled at the irony of taking Steven's punishment yet again and was glad Alder had been interrupted before finishing the job.

'You found out what they were gonna do today, didn't you, and you came back, to let them think they'd a free hand,' Alder said.

'That's about the size of it, Alder.'

'And you came back for the boss too, didn't you.'

'Is he all right?'

'Well—' Alder hunched one bony shoulder and made a little grimace. 'You better come and see.'

In the corridor, Rennie looked at the clock. It was a little after two.

'If you want to help the boss down, I'll hitch up a rig for us,' Alder suggested, but he waited for Rennie to give the OK, a man used to taking orders, not giving them.

'That'd be good. And Alder, is my horse still in the stables?'

'That old buckskin?'

'That's him. Bring him along would you?'

'Glad to,' Alder said and he left by a side door.

Rennie climbed the stairs and found Rutherford in his original bedroom, sitting in a chair by the window, dressed in all but his boots and clearly exhausted. For a minute Rutherford thought Jim was Steven and he reached for the old single-shot pistol he had been hiding, pointing then lowering it in one movement.

'At last,' he said roughly. 'You finally got here.'

'Are you all right?' Rennie asked him, kneeling to pull on his boots for him.

'More to the point, are you?' he asked, noticing the dirty

127

yellow of Rennie's face.

'I'll live,' Rennie said without much conviction. 'Alder has a rig waiting downstairs.'

'I didn't know Alder was still around,' Rutherford said as Rennie struggled with one of the boots that was a little tight. 'I thought they'd got rid of him long ago, just like they got rid of everybody else that was loyal to me. I guess they thought he was too old and dumb to bother with. He just wandered up to the attic and unlocked the door, said he wanted to know what was going on.'

'We were due a break, Tom.'

'We're not out of here yet. Son, I-I'm not sure I can get downstairs.'

'Sure you can, Tom.'

'Yeah but . . . it's taken all my strength just to get this far.'

Seeing that the older man was just tired and had lost his confidence, Rennie turned his head away slightly, as if Rutherford was joshing him.

'Does this mean I've got to carry you?' he enquired.

'Hell, no,' Rutherford said quickly and then, making up his mind to it, 'Come on, let's give it a shot.'

Rennie got an arm around Tom Rutherford and lifted him to his feet, taking all his weight against himself as he half-walked, half-carried him out of the bedroom, out to the corridor, straight into the path of Clara. She was armed with a revolver and she was mad as hell.

'My father isn't well enough to be walking,' she said flatly. 'He ought to be in bed.'

'Well, you ought to know. You put him there,' Rennie's retort came back at her. 'And where are all your hands now?' Clara had been looking at her parent with an odd, flat, dangerous expression, her pupils too big in her eyes, her skin pale and sweating. Now she turned that look on Rennie and it was the hooded look of a snake about to give a lethal strike.

'What did you say to me, pig farmer?'

'I asked what happened to all your men, Miss Rutherford. Didn't they show up at Sam Cutter's place?'

'You warned them,' she said, shocked by it even though Kelly had already surmised as much. 'You got away from Steve and warned them and then deliberately came back to make me think. . . .'

'Yes, I warned them. Now I'm taking your father to a doctor. A real doctor, this time.'

'No, I don't think so,' she said with a slow shake of the head, her lips staying pursed on the word 'so', as she made another little plan in her head.

'Clara,' her father said to her sharply. 'Do you intend to kill both of us?' Her behaviour in the past few months had been a bitter disappointment to him but seeing her now, seeing the lack of any feeling in her eyes except for thwarted self-interest, something was killed in him, paternal feeling or whatever. He felt it die and he looked at a stranger before him. She was just a greedy, rather stupid woman with a gun in her hand.

'What choice have you left me?' she asked him and the gun came up. Rennie moved with the speed of panic and desperation. He turned and threw himself on top of Rutherford and they fell together to the floor, just as the gun went off, the bullet slicing into his back.

Rennie gave a low cry of pain and rolled away from Rutherford, dazed with shock and sudden blood loss. Clara walked slowly towards her father, who lay helplessly now at her feet, his head twisted awkwardly against the wall, his left arm trapped under him so that he was unable to free his single-shot pistol from his belt.

She raised the gun again and Rutherford faced his finish with open eyes and fearless calm. Clara hesitated. Just for a second she remembered whom she was about to kill. Images of a not unhappy childhood flared and died in her brain but what did they count for now? It was only what was happening at this moment, to her, that she cared about. She raised the gun again, aiming for the middle of her father's forehead.

She had forgotten Rennie, back-shot on the floor behind her but he had come to his senses in time to see what she was about to do. In the circumstances he did the only thing he could. He gripped the edge of the rug and jerked as hard as he could, lifting her off her feet and shooting her backwards against the banister. Her arms pinwheeled and she went right over the rail, head first, her indignant, angry scream splitting the air, then a dull crack as she hit the floor, her skull opening like a soft-boiled egg on the stone hallway. Rennie knew without having to look that she was dead.

The two men lying on the floor looked at one another with shocked faces. Nobody spoke and they were in the same positions when Alder appeared at the head of the stairs. He had just seen Clara lying in her own brains and he was half expecting to find Rutherford, Rennie or both of them in the same condition.

'Are you all right there, Mr Rutherford?' he asked, helping him to his feet, while Rennie, with horrible slowness got up on his own. 'What happened?' Alder wanted to know.

'She tried to kill me,' Rutherford said looking sternly at an ashen-faced Rennie.

'God, I'm sorry, Tom. I didn't know what else to do to stop her.'

'You did all right,' Rutherford said and he put a hand on each of Rennie's shoulders, gripping hard. 'What were you thinking about, boy, throwing yourself in front of a goddamned gun like that? Are you hit?' He moved his hands up to Rennie's neck, looking hard but compassionately into the distressed face of the younger man. He ran his hands down his shoulders and arms and then up his sides, his concern turning to alarm when his left hand came away bloody.

'She did hit you!'

'I'm all right, Tom.'

'Christ.' Rutherford made him turn, pulling up his shirt to inspect the wound. The bullet had sliced a deep gouge but had gone in and out cleanly through the fleshy part of his back, hitting nothing vital, nor had it carried shirt material into the wound as the shirt had been loose and had ridden up when he fell.

'It needs to be cleaned and packed. Alder, go down and fetch my medicine chest. It's in the office, you know where, and see if there's any hot water in the kitchen.'

'Sir, we don't have time,' Rennie cut in. 'Kelly and the others—'

'I don't think we'll be seeing them again, Jim. You saw her face. She saw it was all over.'

Rennie shut his eyes for a minute, reliving the moment of her death and that awful scream as she plunged over the railing. When he opened his eyes, both men were watching him.

'Maybe you're right,' he conceded, his brain almost going into a tired stall at the idea of another round with Kelly and Gus and his brother. With a little nod he started to move forward when suddenly his head swam.

'Catch him,' Rutherford shouted urgently, seeing that he was fainting. Instinctively, Alder ducked as Rennie went into a forward roll, taking Jim's weight across his own back and gently lifting him, an arm around his legs.

'Put him in my bed,' Rutherford said. Then he turned to the handrail and looked down to where his daughter lay in a very dead sprawl on the hall floor. He felt an overwhelming swamp of emotions flood over him and then ebb away. He committed all she had been and done to the past and he buried her in his mind. And then he thanked his maker for sending Jim Rennie.

131

CHAPTER NINETEEN

The mock party, staged for the benefit of those Jim Rennie had predicted would come to observe, was over. Sam Cutter stood in shirt sleeves, his dress tie and good Sunday waistcoat both undone, drinking a reviving cup of coffee and surveying the scene in his normally neat, tidy, well-ordered yard.

To the casual observer it might have seemed that a minor Civil War engagement had taken place on this one spot. The trestle tables that had been set out in the morning to carry food and drink looked as if they had been shelled. The food was gone, the beer kegs were empty but the debris remained, a great shambles of plates and cups and bottles and wadded up napkins. Chairs stood about in little groups as if in idle gossip, some of them overturned. There was even a body on the ground, a man lying amongst the litter, asleep, his head cradled on the crook of his arm.

The homesteaders had nervously pretended to enjoy themselves, while waiting for word of their homes and families and when the news had eventually come, that all Jim Rennie's little traps were sprung, that no blood had been shed on the homesteaders' side and that Cass had been alerted and brought back to make sure the would-be arsonists were properly dealt with, they began to celebrate with a vengeance.

It was certainly a day to remember. They had at last got the monkey off their backs and Sam Cutter made sure that everyone acknowledged whom they owed that debt to. Even Tom Colton was forced to admit that it would have been a different story without the personal sacrifice of the man from Creeback. Now Sam picked his way through the litter of the yard, wondering whether that sacrifice had cost his dearest friend his life.

There had been no word from the Rutherford household. Sam had already made up his mind to saddle up and ride out there in a few minutes, just as soon as he found out who was riding down into his yard.

He put his coffee mug down and walked out to meet the lone horseman, an arm raised to shield his eyes from the late, low afternoon sun. When he saw that it was Rennie, riding with a curious list to the side, he felt a tidal surge of relief.

'Well, thank God,' he breathed as the old buckskin drew level with him. 'Thank God you're all right,' he said aloud. Rennie dismounted, holding his right arm awkwardly against himself to prevent any painful stretch in his injured back. For his part he was just as glad to see Sam alive and well.

'Did it work?' he asked with an anxious look around the wrecked and disordered yard. 'Is everything all right?'

'It worked like a charm, hardly anybody hurt. Oh, except for something that happened at Dave Burrows' place. They left their boy John to take care of things and one of the men who turned up to torch the place got shot and the other burned to death. The fellow who got shot was called Sharp. The other one was called Gus. There weren't any casualties on our side. Somebody went after Cass day before yesterday, just like you said. He got here in time to round up every one of them murdering, barn-burning— Well. He was fit to be tied at first, taking the law into our hands and so on, but after he calmed down he saw how it would have turned out if we hadn't done it your way.'

Rennie nodded but it seemed to Sam that he wasn't taking it in. His eyes seemed dulled and heavy.

'What happened with you? What about Rutherford?'

'Oh . . . I had a little help. Rutherford is OK.' Rennie's report was to say the least economical and Sam leaned towards him slightly, waiting for the rest.

'Is that it?'

'Something happened before I left,' Rennie said reluctantly, not wanting to remember what had happened, let alone talk about it.

'What do you mean something happened?'

'Clara came back. She was angry enough for us to work out that she'd been stopped in her tracks.'

'And—' Sam asked urgently, sensing that his friend had been way out on a limb today.

'I killed her, Sam.'

He met Sam's eyes and saw plain shock and surprise, but mostly disbelief.

'What?'

'She was about to kill her father. I hadn't any choice.'

But Sam could see that Rennie had badly wanted there to be another choice, any choice but the one he had taken, to send her crashing to her death, her dying scream still ringing in his head.

Behind them the house door opened and Frances and Eve came down towards them, Frances wearing an apron, all ready for the big clean-up, Eve still wearing her cornflower-blue party dress, her hair swept up in a striking adult style, little pearls on her ears and a flush of angry heat in her cheeks. Unlike Frances, she did not appear glad to see him. Her mother went straight to him and pressed her hand to his face, looking into his eyes with a mother's concern.

'We're so grateful to you, Jim,' she said quietly. He shook his head deprecatingly but was touched by her gesture.

'You promised to feed me if I came back again, remember,' he reminded her. Eve had no words of welcome for him. She began by mimicking her mother.

'We're so grateful to you, Jim,' she said with mock sweetness. 'We're so grateful you went back to that house to let them kill you. As if you wanted them to kill you.'

The fool would never understand what a shock it had been to her that night when her father had told her that he had escaped from those people and then had gone back, quite deliberately. She could scarcely forgive him that.

'I had to go back,' he tried, shocked by her anger.

'You didn't have to. I happen to think. . . .' She faltered. It was hardly the time or place to say it and not in front of her folks but it had to be said. 'I think you're more important than . . . than a railroad, than a strip of dirt and grass. But nobody else seemed to think so or they wouldn't have let you go,' and she glared meaningfully at her father.

'If I hadn't gone back, Eve, Clara Rutherford would have known that I'd warned all of you about her plans for today. She would have changed those plans and one night, when you were all sleeping in your beds, they'd have come and people would have died for nothing, died trying to protect their strip of dirt and grass.'

Eve stubbornly looked away. She did not want to hear his logical arguments. He was too clever with his tongue and too rash with his own life. Did he forget that his fate was now also her fate? She gave him one more hard, unforgiving look but could not sustain it in the face of her worn-down, battle-scarred adversary.

'What you mean is I come last, after settlers and good causes,' she said bitterly and she turned and hurried back to the house at a half-run. Rennie started after her but Sam gently restrained him.

'Let her be for now, Jim. She's just been worried sick about you, same as me. Same as all of us,' he said with a nod to his wife.

'We can't tell you how glad we were to see you come over that hill.'

'I must admit, there were moments when I didn't think I'd ever get this far again.'

'Well, you're here now, there's plenty of food left, fresh coffee on the stove. I think we could even stretch to a hot bath for you,' Frances said invitingly. He nodded his thanks to her and she walked away, thinking he had accepted her offer but Rennie turned to Sam with a question.

'Did he get away?' he asked and Sam didn't need to ask whom he meant.

'Nobody saw hide or hair of him or Kelly all day.'

Rennie nodded to himself, his eyes quietly following the gentle sweep of Sam's horizon. The sun had begun to decline behind the trees and long shadows crept like invaders up to the yard. He felt a chill in the breeze suddenly.

'Think I'll take a rain check on that supper.' Sam moved closer to his friend, the sensation of anxiety that had dogged him all day returning abruptly. It was all over for the settlers but it wasn't over for Rennie.

'He'll be in the next county by now,' Sam said without conviction.

'For his sake I hope he is.' Jim turned to mount up and Sam struggled to find something to say to detain him.

'I wish you wouldn't go like this,' he said, noticing how he seemed to be favouring his right arm and how he bit his lip as he settled back in the saddle. Sam held onto the bridle and Rennie patiently waited, making no move to go. 'I've got all this beer—' He gestured to the remains of the party and the drunk snoring on the ground. Rennie laughed softly and Sam released the bridle.

'I could surely use a drink,' Rennie admitted, 'but I just

want to see how things are at home. I haven't been there since. . . .' He tried to remember. How long ago had it been since his life had been his own? 'Tell Frances thanks anyway,' he said.

Sam watched till he was gone and turned as Frances came back down from the porch to stand beside him.

'Do we have our daughter to thank for that?' she asked with a touch of exasperation.

'No. I think it was something I might have said,' Sam admitted.

On the south side of the ravine, Steven Rennie had settled down behind good cover to watch and wait. He had time to think, plenty of time as he smoked three thin cigarettes all the way down and every once in a while took a satisfying pull from a hip flask. By the time the familiar buckskin horse came down the slope on the other side, the flask was empty and his mouth was stale with tobacco and liquor.

He stepped out of cover and took two or three steps onto the bridge but even so it was a moment before Jim Rennie noticed him. A light touch of the rein brought the buckskin to a halt and he got down carefully, his lower lip nipped between his teeth, the stretching movement as he swung his right leg down causing him considerable discomfort.

'I thought you'd be in the next county by now, Steven,' he said and he slipped his rifle free and gave the horse a little push, sending it back across the bridge a ways.

'So Kelly was right,' Steven said bitterly.

'Oh? What was Kelly right about this time?'

'He said you warned them, warned the soddies.'

Jim Rennie made no reply. He had lived through one of the longest days of his life today and even yet he could hear Clara scream as she plunged headfirst over the balcony. And now here was his brother, still here even though it should have been obvious, even to him, that the jig was up. He looked angrier than a hornet and he'd been drinking. The smell of the liquor was powerful in the still, hot afternoon air.

'Why don't you just get out of here while you still can,' he advised, moving closer to the centre of the bridge. One of his boots needed mending and the worn-down heel rang out metallically as he walked. 'Turn around and walk away and don't come back.'

'Or what? Are you going to turn me in?' Steven asked, with an arrogant, cocky tilt of the head and a particularly baiting tone of voice which had always aggravated his brother in the past and had, on more than one occasion when they were boys, led to blows. 'We have something to settle, you and me.'

'I've got no quarrel with you, Steven. You played your hand here and you lost.'

'Because of you.'

'Clara's dead and so is Gus. Kelly hasn't been seen—'

'Now wait. Wait a minute.' Steven held up two hands as if to prevent something from rolling over him. 'I spoke to Clara a couple of hours ago.'

'She's dead, Steven. Your meal ticket is dead. So is Gus. A sixteen-year-old boy torched him when he tried to burn down his parents' house.'

'You bastard.'

'Which leaves your old friend Kelly. Where is Kelly, Steven? Did he send you down here? You get all the really important jobs, huh?'

Rennie drew in a long breath, filling his chest, then let it out in a tired trickle, figuring that now he had laid it out for Steven he would do the smart thing and go. He half-turned, looked back at Steven, who was staring down at the ground, hands on hips, fingers spaced wide, breathing hard.

'Be grateful you got out of this one without a jail sentence.'

Rennie turned away from his brother and started walking back towards his horse, who had wandered right back to where bushes edged the road and was noisily cropping on the leaves. He could have whistled and he would have come, but Rennie suddenly knew that his brother was not going to leave it alone and he gave him his chance.

He heard a soft, quick step behind him, saw the shadow of a raised fist and he braced himself, planting his feet and when Steven was right up close, jabbed the rifle back into his brother's rib cage. He turned as his brother doubled over and with one clean, unbroken movement brought the rifle stock up under Steven's chin. There was a crack as walnut connected with bone and Rennie was hit with a fine spray of blood from Steven as a tooth splintered and blood flooded from his mouth. He stumbled against the bridge parapet, moaning in pain, his forearm pressed to his mouth to staunch the blood. Rennie moved in again and disarmed Steven, lifting his pistol from his belt and throwing it out over the drop, then, breathing hard himself, he leaned for a moment against the parapet, his rifle on Steven.

'Are we done now?' Jim asked, drawing another ragged breath down, each breath beginning to hurt, his back on fire with the exertion.

Steven fought to staunch the bleeding, finding a neckerchief in his pocket, still surprised that his brother had anticipated him. He looked up at him with dull hatred and realized that he had never felt any other way about him. From the first he could recall he had been angry with him and jealous of the calm, deliberate, competent way he led his life. Even when he had persuaded Clara to let Jim live, he had not really meant it, had enjoyed seeing him embattled, physically hurt, just as he had enjoyed it at Fort Macauley. There was no point in pretending now.

'You're just a goddamned thorn in my side,' Steven said aloud.

'Nobody asked you to come here. Why do you always blame

everybody else for your stupidity?'

'Don't call me stupid,' Steven bellowed and with that he charged, taking Jim completely by surprise.

He had time to squeeze off one shot before Steven hit him like a charging bull and they toppled to the ground together, rolling to the centre of the bridge, pummelling one another with tight, blocked-in punches, first Jim on top and then Steven, who got in one or two good blows before Jim managed to get his knee under his brother's crotch and levered him off, getting in a punch to the side of his head on the way.

Steven landed awkwardly on his right elbow and let out a scream of angry pain, thinking for a minute that he had broken it.

Jim sat up dizzily and looked around for the rifle, which he had dropped and which had been kicked in the scuffle to the edge of the bridge. As he rose to his feet, the pain in his back became suddenly unbearable and he staggered to the parapet, holding on for dear life as the whole canyon below him went into a sickening spin. Then the ringing in his head stopped and he bent down to pick up the rifle, got hands to it, but got no further.

Steven had discovered that though painful and starting to swell alarmingly, his arm was not broken and with a grunt of relief he got to one knee, ready to fight on.

Then he saw a patch of blood on the bridge, fresh and warm still and he looked up to see his brother almost fainting by the railing, with a plate-sized circle of blood on his back. He felt a rush of triumph as he stood, took two swift steps up to Jim and then felled him with a crippling blow to the wound on his back. Jim made no sound as he went down, his face ashen, his head rolling slackly to one side.

Panting a little and sweating, blood still filling his mouth from that earlier blow, Steven stepped over his brother and looked quickly both ways, with the sudden certainty in his head that a horde of angry homesteaders were about to descend on him. But the trail in both directions was empty and the only sound was his own breathing, harsh and agitated. He worked his tongue against the damaged tooth and rocked it loose, spat it out and cleaned his raw mouth on his sleeve and then after filling his chest again and again, he bent over his brother.

His arm hurt like hell but he almost enjoyed it as he helped Jim Rennie to his feet, supporting him around the waist and half carrying him to the bridge railing. He let his weight fall forwards slightly and he showed him the view. It had always been impressive, an awesome gash in the smooth contour of the land, the black belly of the ravine sending up a hot updraught.

Desperately Jim tried to collect his scattered wits. He fought down hot sickness and shook his head repeatedly to clear it, while below him the bridge and the ravine spun slowly like a carousel.

Steven took a good grip on the back of Rennie's belt and lifted him onto the handrail, stomach across, head hanging down. The drop seemed to his distorted perspective like a mile of revolving blackness, with a stale, hot odour catching the back of his throat. He expected to die now, to plunge down onto the rocks and boulders strewn across the canyon floor. What an irony, he thought, to die like Clara, only this will take a second or two longer, but you'll scream just like her. He was helpless to prevent Steven's attempts to send him over. He felt cold suddenly too and somewhere at the back of his mind a warning flashed about that. He had heard men say they were cold, in the war, after enduring some hellish wound and then they usually died, from blood loss or shock or both.

Somehow he did not want to die at his brother's hand and he assuredly did not want to die on those rocks that lay like broken teeth in the shadows below.

Steven was grunting with the effort. He swung a leg over the parapet and straddled it to get better purchase. Jim's two legs went over, but with a frantic twist of the body he managed to grip the rail with one hand and Steven's shirt with the other.

He looked up and met his brother's eyes. There was something hellishly cold about the stare he met, blank, indifferent, mindless and Rennie realized that his young brother, whom he had protected and shielded and kept out of all kinds of trouble all his life, was as black-hearted as Clara and twice as dangerous as Gus and Kelly.

'Let me go, damn you,' Steven swore, fighting to free the hand gripping him, a hand that felt like a lump of ice. Rennie channelled all the strength he had left into the arm he had hooked around the railing, just as Steven dug his fingers into Rennie's throat and tried to push him back. His mouth working with pent-up rage, he leaned way out, bludgeoning his brother away from the hold he had on life.

But just as Jim felt his hold slipping, his strength ebbing, he remembered that Steven had an injury too and he took an enormous gamble. He let go of his shirt and reached for his injured arm, gripping the elbow and twisting as hard as he was able.

It was over in a second. The fierce jolt of pain that shot up Steven's arm made him let go his hold on his brother as he instinctively drew back to protect himself and with a startled look he overbalanced. He swayed almost lazily away from his brother until gravity took over, his legs unlocking, and he fell, diving down into the darkness. There was a muffled thud and a rumble or two of displaced rocks and then silence.

Rennie had no memory of reaching the safety of the bridge. He simply found himself standing with his back against the handrail, numbed by Steven's brutality and shocked by his death. But slowly, as he turned to look down at what lay on the floor of the ravine, what he felt most of all was relief. He had survived all that they had done to him and lived to tell the tale. Clara was dead, Gus burned to a crisp like all the homes he had torched in the last few months, and Steven was at the bottom of the ravine. He wouldn't have taken any bets on that outcome a week ago.

He looked up from wondering how he was going to retrieve his brother's body just as the buckskin came wandering towards him, curious now that the scuffle was over, rubbing his nose on Rennie's arm like an overgrown dog. Rennie took the reins and started for home. Steven would have to keep for another day.

CHAPTER TWENTY

Rennie entered Creeback valley walking, not even leading the buckskin, who wandered along behind him, ears pricked, sensing that he was home at last. Warm, late afternoon light lay kindly on the shingled roof of the house and on the sturdy outline of the Dutch barn. He had planted vegetables off to one side of the house and the recent rain had brought them on to gratifying size. You could grow anything in this valley, with its sheltering slopes and southern tilt. You could spend your life here and never grow tired of the sight of it. But as Jim Rennie walked home that day he hardly raised his eyes to the valley he loved and his thoughts were of another home, one he had not seen since 1865. He paid no mind to the pasture and the brook and the gentle swell of the hills, for his mind was seeing Boston Commons and the Charles River. He would have to go home. He would have to tell his mother that her younger boy was dead. Maybe he would even find the courage to explain to his father that he had killed him.

He stopped to unsaddle the buckskin, putting the saddle and gear on the corral rail and turning the horse into the corral. The buckskin looked at him speculatively for a while, wondering why he was being penned up today when he usually got to run free on the pasture. Rennie leaned his chest on the corral pole and looked tiredly back at him.

144

'Not today. I'm too tired to go chasing after you if you decide to take off into the hills.' The buckskin poked a coaxing nose over the rail, blowing Rennie's dirty hair. 'Not today, boy. We both need a little rest, I think.' Rennie laughed and rubbed the horse's blunt, silky nose but even as he stood by the corral, Rennie could feel pain and heat in the wound in his back and the beginning of a trickle of blood again. But the mare and foal had to be seen to and he turned to check on them.

As he approached the barn door something made him pause and turn to look back at the horse in the corral and then up to the house. Had there been something just then, a glint perhaps of sun on metal or an odd noise? He held his breath and stood stock still for a moment or two and then concluding that it was nothing, just his own overwound state he turned to the warm darkness of the barn and walked straight into the butt of a rifle, travelling towards him at speed.

Kelly stood over Rennie's fallen body, his blue eyes for once bereft of humour. For a minute he debated simply shooting him where he lay but that would be too quick, too merciful.

He bound Rennie by the wrists, threw the end of the rope over a roof beam and then hauled on the rope till his heels were swinging clear of the floor by a good six inches. He tied off the rope and fetched a bucket of water from the trough by the corral, threw the water over Rennie and watched him revive.

He walked slowly around his prisoner and saw for the first time the little patch of blood on his shirt, under the shoulder blade. He pulled the shirt free to have a better look and saw Alder's fairly expert packing over the freshly bleeding bullet wound. He circled on around and fetched up in front of Rennie, waiting with feline patience for him to get the

picture. When he saw Rennie's eyes brighten with compre-
hension, he moved around in back of him again.

'Did she do that to you?' he asked softly. 'Did she shoot you
before you killed her, you bastard?' And he hit Rennie with
the rifle stock, square against the wound, sending a shock
wave of pain through him. For a second Rennie was badly
winded, unable to drag enough air down into his chest, then
when he finally could it burned worse than hell.

'How much did it hurt, Rennie?' Kelly remorselessly
questioned him. 'Do you think it hurt her as much as this?'

The second blow was delivered with a clenched fist and
while not nearly as bad as the rifle, it still hurt almost beyond
endurance. Rennie's brain raced, looking for a way to fight
back, to stop his own destruction, but he could already taste
the bitterness of losing to Kelly, after winning out over
everything else.

Because Kelly was on a righteous crusade. He had seen the
woman he wanted, loved, in his own way, intended to bind to
him, lying dead on the floor, had overheard some of what
happened to her as he let himself in the back way to get some
extra cartridges and a couple of glasses of brandy. He could
have taken the old man and Alder but stayed his hand. He
would go back later and take care of everything. For now he
simply wanted to revenge himself on Rennie, wanted to
destroy him for taking away Kelly's only chance of a
prosperous, cushioned, comfortable existence with a woman
he could tolerate. She wasn't a whore, she wasn't his mother,
she was ballsy and smart and she liked it when he was a little
rough with her. And as he stacked up all that she had been
and all that he had now lost – because without her the ranch
and the money and all that the railroad would bring were lost
to him – he felt a terrific surge of fury build in him.

He bowed his head to let it subside a little, otherwise he
would have gutted Rennie there and then, and he let the heat

of it cool just enough to let him think. Rennie raised his head and looked him right in the eye.

'She called you a useless, lazy bum before she died, if it makes you feel any better,' Rennie said, with as much of a shrug as he could assay with his arms stretched over his head. The lie pierced Kelly like a knife and for a second his vision blurred, his mouth slacked open helplessly and he gave a hoarse cry, pushing his face up against Rennie.

'Liar!'

'Why do you care so much, Kelly? She was just another meal ticket, right?'

'She was going to be my wife, you murdering asshole.'

Rennie stared at Kelly for a minute, then he started to laugh. He laughed till the muscles in his neck went into spasm and he had to let his head roll forward to ease the pain. Sweat ran heavy from his brow and nose, dripping like rain on his shirt.

'You poor deluded sap. You thought Clara Rutherford, the toast of Paris and New York, was ever going to marry you?'

'Why the hell not?'

'Because you were *her* meal ticket.'

Kelly's mouth worked and his eyes jumped from Rennie to the ground and back again. He shifted his feet and tried to think.

'How's that again?'

Rennie felt his pulse slow just a shade. He had taken the heat out of the situation a little, bought some valuable time, but where it was going to get him, he had no idea.

'She told me as much, called you and Steven her hired dog and pony. You were there to get her what she wanted. Then when she was done with you, she would have sent you packing.'

'It wasn't like that, you lyin' no-account. She never told you nothin'.

147

'Have it your way, Kelly. But you're wasting a lot of good anger on a woman who didn't care for anybody but herself.'

And all at once Kelly saw through him, saw what he was trying to do. His head cleared of any doubt and he gave a soft laugh.

'That was real clever, Captain. I almost bought it too. You make me despise her and then I realize that you've done us both a favour, is that it? What the hell, the bitch deserved it, right?' Kelly said in a different voice, a calm and cold voice that left Rennie without any hope. He tried to swallow, but nothing in the chest and neck area seemed to be working properly. Kelly was in charge of the situation again; his mind was made up to whatever it was he intended doing and nothing Rennie could say now would alter that. He tried to brace himself, both physically and mentally but felt so tired and weary that he could barely draw a deep breath.

Kelly had moved away and was looking in at the mare and her foal, his mouth pursed slightly. He strolled back towards Rennie, stood before him to savour the moment and then reached into his pocket for a match. Rennie closed his eyes. When he looked again, Kelly was lighting the storm lantern, holding it high till the glass started to get warm, then he tossed it into some hay bales, watched to make sure the flames took hold, and then with a lazy smile, turned and walked away.

Rennie started to struggle, trying to free his hands from the rope that was all but cutting off his circulation, trying to swing his legs up towards the stretch of retaining rope in an attempt to bump it free. But he could make no headway and suddenly he took in a lungful of acrid smoke and started a retching cough that he could not control. With his arms stretched above his head, he found he could not fill his lungs properly. He glanced at the barn door and saw Kelly standing there watching him; then he turned and strolled out into the yard.

Rennie felt himself starting to pass out. He could not breathe or see and as his head rolled forward, he heard the mare and her foal start to panic with the increasing heat and smoke, squealing and kicking the sides of the stall to get free. Those pitiful cries and his own rasping breaths were the last things Rennie heard before the heat and smoke engulfed him.

Kelly rode at a clip up the valley trail and turned for Alexander, slowing only when he was close to Sandy Creek. He was almost home free, paused for a minute before starting down the gradient to the bridge to look back to see if there was any visible sign of smoke. There was none to be seen and he shrugged and turned back, to find his path obstructed by three riders. He had no idea where they had come from. They sat in silence, watching him, making no move to let him pass, and only when he forced his horse forward to try to push through did they move, forming a little square around him.

It was over in a moment. A gun was rammed hard into the bone under his left ear and his arms were bound up tight with a clean, new rope. They gave him no time to struggle, no chance to fight. He was disarmed and trussed with rough speed and his curses and shouts were cut off with a wadded up kerchief, which was bound tight around his jaw.

Under a tree close to the spot where Kelly had knifed the boy to death, the little party came to rest, the three men in sober, expensive, black suits, Kelly bound and gagged. Another rope was produced, a thicker one, also new. This one went over a tree branch and then around Kelly's neck.

His eyes were wild with fury, indignation and confusion. He did not recognize the three men, could not remember what indiscretion from his past had brought them here. They were about to hang him and he did not know why. The location had no significance for him. He had shed a man's blood here and then had put it out of his mind.

One of the men reached over and took off Kelly's gag but given the chance to speak, he remained stubbornly silent, glaring at each of them as if to burn their faces into his memory. He noticed that they all looked alike, the same dark hair and dark blue eyes, the same short, blunt noses.

In the silence, a breeze stirred the canopy of trees overhead with a dry sighing and one of the horses stooped to crop the grass noisily. One of the men took something from his pocket and held it up to let Kelly see what it was, and all at once he knew that this was all about Ben Corey. These men were somehow connected to him and they had got hold of Jim Rennie's evidence, the cheap metal cross he had lost here that day, lost it in a brief struggle with the boy when he realized that Kelly had brought him here to murder him.

'My name is Arthur Anderson,' one of the men finally spoke. 'These are my brothers, Alexander, Junior and Robert.'

Kelly knew who they were now; big shots in Alexander, sons of the man who had founded the town, named half the goddamned town after himself.

'Whoever you are, you've made a big mistake here. You better cut me loose before you buy yourself a whole load of trouble.' Kelly warned them, twisting his arms against the over-tight bindings. The three men looked back at him coldly, unmoved by his warning.

'A boy died here,' Arthur continued, nodding towards the steep drop to his left. Kelly followed his gaze and remembered watching the boy tumble down the slope. He cursed himself now for not waiting to watch him hit the water and it occurred to him that if the boy had floated away downstream, none of this would have happened.

'He was our nephew,' Arthur Anderson said. 'We found this in his coffin, where Jim Rennie hid it when he came to pay respects to our sister. We know that it was his evidence that you killed the boy.'

150

'It doesn't belong to me. I never owned any such thing,' Kelly defiantly told them, his voice rising a little.

'Well, quite a few people have told us otherwise, Mr Kelly. But we, my brothers and I, have discussed it and we're agreed that it might be difficult to prove in a court of law.'

Kelly let a sigh trickle from his nostrils and shifted more comfortably in the saddle. Men like this always did what was right.

'Let me loose and I'll say nothin' about what you did to me today,' he said reasonably. 'I didn't harm the boy. We can go our separate ways and nothin' said about it.'

Silence. The three men looked at him with the same cold, hard, unrelenting eyes, minds already made up to it and Kelly did not know what else to do to make them turn from this path. He saw no parallel between his own plight and that of Jim Rennie, trussed and helpless in a burning barn not half an hour since.

'This is what we think happened.' Arthur said quietly, leaning forward in the saddle as if to confide in Kelly. 'My nephew received a telegram from Washington about a railroad coming this way next year or the next, a telegram which your employer asked him to bring to her personally if it came and which she did not want the world to know about, not yet anyway. Then she told you to take care of the boy on the way back to town, which you did here on this track.'

Arthur leaned back in the saddle and felt a great stab of grief for that young nephew of his, such a pleasant, likeable boy, the apple of his mother's eye.

'You ended his young life here, Mr Kelly, on the word of Clara Rutherford and you ended it for nothing. Because there isn't going to be a railroad. Miss Rutherford got her facts wrong. Her information came from an unreliable source in Washington. All this for nothing, you miserable, low down filthy—'

'Arthur,' one of his brothers steadied him, a hand on his shoulder. They had decided at the start that they would remain cool, and carry out their task in a disciplined fashion. They were going to lynch him, but they were no lynch mob. This was an execution and it would be done right.

'We've gathered all our evidence, Mr Kelly, and we've decided you are guilty and you will hang, here, today, on this spot where in cold blood you took the life of our nephew, Benjamin Corey. Is there anything you want to say?'

Kelly looked at their faces and knew that this was it. No one was coming to rescue him, no one would care. He had killed the boy and he had enjoyed it and now these men wanted payment.

'He died fightin',' he said, looking at each face before him and each man felt a touch of gratitude, though none showed it. It was possibly the only decent thing Kelly had ever done in his life and as the horse was led away from under him and the rope tightened and cut off his air, his last thought was to wonder why he should want to make those men feel better about Corey's death.

The three brothers watched the body kick and then swing and then hang still until there was no life left and then they cut him down. They untied him and between the three of them, tossed him over the edge of the drop and watched him smash into the rocks before sliding into the water and spinning away downstream, just as Corey should have done. They returned to their horses and rode back to the trail and in single file wound their way down into Sandy Creek, crossing the little bridge over the river and pausing just for a second to make sure that Kelly was gone before riding on into town.

CHAPTER
TWENTY-ONE

Rennie's hearing returned, but not his vision at first and so he found himself trying to understand what was happening by just identifying voices. First there was Sam.

'Tom, put those over there and ... plenty of water on them, that's it. Andy, son, those are hot, be careful. Can somebody tether Jim's horse? Don't know why he doesn't just get a dog, damned horse thinks it's a dog.'

'Think we got it under control, Sam.' That was Tom Colton, breathing hard and breaking into a retching cough at the end, then a voice Jim Rennie could not identify.

'There isn't any coffee in the house. No coffee, for Pete's sake.'

'Coffee in my saddle-bags, Joe,' Tom Colton shouted.

Then he felt something wonderfully cold on his face and head, the water trickling into his mouth and eyes and caking the dirt and soot on his face and throat. It was water from the little stream at the edge of the meadow, sweet and cool. Only one person would have thought of going there for it. Frances Cutter raised his head a little and pressed the cold cloth to the back of his neck.

'Come on, sweetheart. Give me a nice big breath.' She

wrung the cloth out in the bucket of clean water and squeezed it out over his brow and lips again and slowly he started to become aware of where he was. He could feel hard ground under his legs and back but his shoulders and head rested on something soft and yielding. He was being cradled on someone's knees, their hands, at first resting on his shoulders, began to smooth his hair off his brow, lifting each individual strand of hair with fingers that trembled slightly. There was a snuffling, hiccoughing sound accompanying this and then a soft cheek was pressed to his face and a tender kiss was placed on his mouth.

'Eve, honey, let the man breath,' Sam said, his voice a little bit exasperated, and with that Jim Rennie started to cough. Sam turned him quickly onto his side as he retched up smoke and soot and little slivers of straw and what felt like the lining of his throat and lungs, while his eyes streamed as if with acid. Somebody rubbed his back and the cold cloth was applied again to his forehead, which felt as if it was about to explode, and after a time, his breathing returned to normal. Soot had puddled under his nose and his eyes were bloodshot and still streaming, but at least now he could see, if not that clearly.

Sam was on his left, still shouting orders to a dozen or more men who had been trying to kill the fire in the barn. Hay bales and gear were strewn all around the yard, smoke rising from everything, acrid and bitter. The mare and her foal were both safe in the corral and Andy Cutter was patiently leading the buckskin to the opposite side of the yard to tether him. He was quietly astonished to see them here, helping him now, fighting his fire.

Frances, kneeling on his left, lifted a cup of water to his lips and he drank it all as if his throat was on fire.

'It was Kelly. He was waiting,' he rasped, his voice like gravel sieved over sandpaper.

'Yeah, we saw him riding towards town, just as we got here.'

154

Sam began to explain, seeing that Rennie was having difficulty speaking. 'Just after you left us, I got a bad feeling. Just knew something wasn't right with you. 'Course, I wasn't to know you'd been shot in the back,' he said with heavy irony and a bewildered glance at his wife and daughter. That had come as quite a shock to Sam, when they fought their way into the smoke-filled barn to cut him down and carry him out into the yard, to turn him over and find a bleeding bullet wound.

'Tom Colton and a few others had just come back to help us clear up after the shindig, so I told them I was worried about you, told them I thought your brother and maybe others weren't finished with their dirty work yet, so we saddled up and came right after you.'

'Thank the Lord we did,' Frances murmured, stroking his cheek and forehead.

'We sent Ed Hunter after Kelly, at a distance, just to see where he went. I hope he's all right. He's been gone a while now. But we haven't seen hide nor hair of your brother, Jim.'

Rennie shut his eyes and rolled his head away from Sam, remembering all at once the final minutes on the bridge with his brother, the second death that day that he was directly responsible for. His colour turned grey and Sam looked up at the two women with concern. Tom Colton had come close to look down at Rennie, his head cocked as he gauged the look of the man on the ground.

'Looks like he needs a doctor,' he observed and a voice spoke quietly behind him, so that everybody turned to look.

'I'm a doctor.' He was a man of average build and height, with dark brown hair greying at the temples, a small tidy moustache that was entirely grey and smoke-blue eyes that were familiar to everyone there. He was dressed in a good suit and the watch-chain on his vest had the dull gleam of solid gold.

Sam got to his feet, his expression changing to one of

dawning recognition. He had met this man once before, some years ago.

'It's Sergeant Cutter, isn't it?' the stranger asked, extending a hand. Sam took a grip on the other man's hand, a broad grin on his face now.

Rennie had opened his eyes again and was squinting up with blurred vision and a ringing in his head at the man in the good suit, who knelt down on the ground now to take a closer look at the patient. With a large, blunt-fingered hand, he took a radial pulse, counting off the seconds on his watch, while the man on the ground stared at him, scarce believing what he saw.

'Looks like me and your mother got here just in time,' Lucas Rennie said softly, smiling at his son, brushing the hair back from his dirty forehead.

CHAPTER
TWENTY-TWO

In the concealing darkness of the corral, Jim Rennie coaxed a gentle brush through the coat of the buckskin, stroking his chest with one hand and brushing with the other, while the old horse whickered his pleasure, even though the brushing movement was causing a drag on the wound in his back. In fact his whole body felt like a giant bruise.

'Now I know how you feel,' he said, stroking the ball of his thumb over one of the old horse's scars, a particularly vicious, curving wound that must have been agony to endure. 'Or maybe not. I'm not suffering from anything that won't heal,' he apologized to the large, expressive brown eyes that watched him patiently, though he knew that statement wasn't true.

It was all over everyone kept saying. Even Kelly, who had so nearly ended it for him today, was dead, according to Ed Hunter, who had described the scene he had witnessed on the track at Sandy Creek with a touch of reverence. Kelly's past had finally caught up with him, a retribution so exact and clinical it had left all those Ed described it to wishing they had seen it for themselves. So now it really was all over, except that it never would be. It would always be with him, like the war, like Fort Macaulay. His brain would roll the dead out at unexpected moments for the rest of his life.

'It's nice to be home though, huh?' he murmured. He turned slightly so that he could see the house. The windows were open and lamplight and a mingling of voices spilled out onto the porch.

He tried to separate them. He could hear Sam and his father, discussing the war, their voices overlapping, enthusiastic, agreeing and disagreeing amicably. In the background he could hear Frances and his mother, though not the subject matter. His mother always spoke quite slowly, her tone full of gentle humour. He felt his heart give a painful squeeze to hear her. Still, hours later, he could not credit that they were both here, had trekked half-way across the country to see him, to find out for themselves if he were all right. They had brought Meg with them, the girl who had come to the family as a fourteen-year-old servant. She had refused to let them make the journey alone and had invited herself along to take care of the pair of them. His reunion with Meg had been almost more emotional than with his mother. She had gathered him into her embrace and stroked his head and face as if he were the baby he had been when she arrived in the Rennie household.

'There now, there now,' she kept saying, unable to stop staring lovingly at him, the man who had been the boy she had loved as her own.

His mother more or less stopped breathing for the long minute that she held him, her heart full, her throat too clogged to speak, while his father, giving him a gentle squeeze around the waist, mindful of his injury, looked into his eyes and saw deeper than any, the fresh scarring of the last few days.

'We'll talk later,' was all he said, and Rennie knew he would tell his father everything, even how Steven died, but not tonight.

They had supper together, food brought by Frances,

alcohol supplied by the doctor, brought from Boston as a gift.

Lucas Rennie denied they had travelled all this way just to see their son, but had come at the invitation of Doctor Garson, who had written to the hospital in Boston where he taught surgery, asking for the names of any doctors who might want to come out West to practise. Alexander was growing fast and they desperately needed at least one other medical man. Lucas Rennie had decided to come see for himself before committing any of his colleagues or students to such an enterprise. His wife shook her head and smiled at him.

'Lucas Rennie, you are such a liar.'

'I beg your pardon, Mary my dear, but I am not.'

'Well I came to see my son,' she said, with a fond look towards him. 'Came to find out if he was well and happy and to see if the girl he speaks about so often in his letters was anywhere near as pretty as he told us.'

All eyes suddenly turned towards Eve and she blushed and put a hand up to her throat, then the back of her neck and then looked imploringly at Jim, but there was to be no help from that quarter.

'Just a few hours ago she told me she never wanted to see me again,' he said in an injured tone and received a wadded up napkin in the face for his pains.

'And I meant it too,' she laughed, and everyone else laughed with her.

Now it was late and the women were clearing up, the men putting the world to rights and he had come out to see to the buckskin and to get a little air. He heard the creak of the corral gate and turned to find Eve before him, arms folded, her expression serious.

'I'm sorry I spoke to you the way I did this afternoon, Jim. I didn't really mean it.'

'I know,' he almost growled at her, gathering her into his

arms and pressing his face into her hair.

'If you knew how it felt when Dad told me you'd gone. . . .'

'How did it feel?' he asked, raising his head to look down at her.

'Like you were already dead and I might as well be dead too.'

He kissed her, taking his time, tasting her, wanting never to let her out of his sight.

'Will you marry me?' he asked her when he had made her too breathless to reply. She nodded vigorously, slipped her arms around his waist and her hands down the back of his jeans and rested her cheek against the warm column of his throat.

'I thought you'd never ask.'

On the porch, the Cutters and Jim's parents had come out to take the air too and saw the exchange between their children in the corral.

'They're always doin' that,' Andrew complained sleepily. His father sat down on the one of the porch chairs and gathered his son up onto his knee.

'Time we were getting you home, young fella.'

At the porch rail Mary Rennie turned with a knowing look towards her husband. Then she leaned towards Frances, slipping her arm around the other woman's waist.

'Frances, I think we'll have to see about getting those banns read first thing tomorrow,' she said and Frances laughed softly and patted the other woman's hand.

'First thing,' she agreed happily.